SCOTT SAPPHIRE
AND THE EMERALD ORCHID

Geoffrey Knight

Storm Moon Press
Exceptional authors. Exceptional stories.

Storm Moon Press LLC
12814 University Club Drive, #102
Tampa, FL 33612

Publishing History
Dare Empire eMedia Productions / 2012
Storm Moon Press / 2013

Cover art by Dare Empire eMedia Productions

ISBN-13   978-1-937058-93-7

ISBN-10   1-937058-93-X

Chapter I

Venice, Italy

The distant song of a gondolier—a happy, melodramatic solo of La Traviata's Libiamo Ne' Lieti Calici, as only a gondolier can do it justice—echoed through the canals and drifted through the open balcony doors of the stranger's hotel room, but Jake Stone didn't even hear it. All he heard was his own desperate panting, the rush of adrenalin in his temples, the pounding of his heart, the wet, hungry sounds of lips crushing and sucking, tongues exploring and licking and diving in deep.

The young man on the receiving end of Jake's wild, ravenous kisses was handsome, and his cock was just as hard as Jake's. His hair was as black as a moonless night, the kind of night that was perfect for a crime. His eyes were so blue, so piercing; if they had been jewels, they would have fetched a fortune.

But Jake was in Venice for a different kind of treasure.

And this beautiful young specimen of a man was going to help him get his hands on it—without even knowing.

In the meantime—

Jake forced the handsome young man backward, their hips

pushing and grinding against one another. Both men were still dressed, each wearing a suit jacket, shirt, tie, trousers with a straining bulge in the crotch. Jake fumbled with the stranger's tie, at the same time shoving him hard against the hotel room dresser.

The open bottle of 1995 *Clos du Mesnil* Krug Champagne that they had ordered from room service took the force of the blow, teetering and swirling before dropping off the edge of the dresser. It had been sitting beside a silver tray containing two crystal flutes and the plate of *Doux Baiser* Belgian chocolates.

In a flash, the blue-eyed man's hand shot out and caught the bottle of champagne, not clumsily by the neck of the bottle, but gracefully by its solid round base, his movement so swift, so smooth, Jake raised an eyebrow, impressed.

"We don't want to waste that," the young man said in an accent that may have been British. Or American. Or something entirely different.

Having caught the bottle, the black-haired man took the opportunity to top up the two champagne glasses on the silver tray. He took a sip of his own before sharing it with Jake, and then placed the glass back on the tray and said, "Might I suggest we head in the opposite direction to avoid anymore potential spills?"

With that, he shoved Jake hard, his body weight and strength arguably equal to that of Jake's, forcing him backward toward the bed.

The back of Jake's legs hit the edge of the mattress.

He felt himself falling backward.

Suddenly, the young man caught him by his tie.

It snapped tight, catching Jake on a 45 degree angle, suspending him between the bed and the man he wanted in it. As he teetered there—like a bottle of champagne caught at the last second—all Jake could ask was, "Who the hell are you?"

The blue-eyed man smiled. "My name's Scott. Scott Sapphire. I work in Mergers & Acquisitions, here on business. But that doesn't mean I can't be distracted by a little pleasure." His free hand seized Jake by his throbbing crotch, squeezing it hard as he sized it up with a smile. "Or should I say, a rather large pleasure."

He let go of both crotch and tie at the same time and let Jake bounce onto the bed. Instantly, Scott climbed on top, straddling Jake's powerful body, their crotches once again writhing and pushing into one another.

Desperately Jake wanted—needed—to be naked.

But Scott was already on the case, hauling and tugging at Jake's tie, pulling it free. He snapped Jake's jacket off, shoulders first, before stripping it from both arms. He hurled it across the room. It snagged briefly on the handle of the open bathroom door before parachuting to the classically tiled Venetian floor.

Scott ripped open Jake's shirt, and two buttons shot through the air.

His reckless desire made Jake even hornier. He grabbed the raven locks of Scott's hair and thrust his tongue even deeper in the young businessman's wet, wild mouth.

When he finally came up for air Jake said, "I'm supposed to wear this shirt to an exhibition opening in an hour's time."

Scott responded by taking the shirt in both hands once again and tearing it open all the way, buttons firing across the room like bullets. "Don't worry, I have plenty of shirts. You can have one of mine." Approvingly, he eyed Jake's now exposed torso, his sparsely-haired muscled chest, his heaving abs. "You look like you're just about my size."

Jake smiled. He had thought exactly the same thing the minute he'd first laid eyes on the handsome stranger three hours earlier in the Piazza San Marco.

Jake had been sitting at a table sipping coffee, eying off the waiters, the tourists, any man who met his checklist.

Around six feet tall.

Short black hair.

Blue eyes.

Broad shoulders.

Just like Jake himself.

Suddenly, a few feet in front of him, a storm of pigeons took to the late afternoon skies as a smartly-dressed stranger in a suit stumbled on a crack in one of the piazza's pavers and fell right toward Jake.

Jake leaped up from his chair and caught the man just before he crashed to the ground.

"*Grazie.*"

"You're welcome."

"You're American," the stranger observed.

You're perfect, Jake thought.

Now in a hotel room of the *Casanova Hotel* in Castello, a short walk from the piazza, Jake sat up, his shirt ripped open, and grinned. "Plenty, you say?" With that he seized Scott's shirt by the collar and ripped with all his strength, wrenching it open from his neck to the belt of his trousers, leaving nothing but Scott's flapping pink tie to cover his smooth, perfectly-sculpted torso.

At the same time, Jake unsnapped Scott's belt and unzipped the businessman's trousers. The thick, pumping shape of Scott's large, hungry cock tried with all its might to break through the fabric of his briefs.

Jake grabbed it in his fist, feeling the stiff meat fill his palm.

Scott grabbed Jake by his shirt and hauled him up and over, the two of them rolling straight off the bed.

Scott landed on his back.

Jake thudded on top of him.

For a moment Jake thought his weight may have winded the beautiful stranger. "Are you—"

There was no need for concern. No time for talk.

Scott grabbed the back of Jake's head and pulled him down into a kiss.

Both men began kicking off their shoes.

Scott was wrestling with Jake's belt now.

Jake was yanking awkwardly, trying to get the rest of his already ripped shirt off his back with one hand.

His other hand slipped loose Scott's tie.

In the next moment, they were both sliding their trousers and briefs down their thick thighs.

At last the thick, sizzling-hot trunks of their cocks met.

Their shafts instantly stabbed into their panting stomachs, jousting and jabbing to the accompaniment of Jake's and Scott's pleasure-filled grunts.

With his back flat to the floor, Scott raised both legs and locked them tight around Jake's bare ass.

Jake began to push his hips down harder, pinning Scott to the floor with no hope of escape, until—

"Condom," Scott said.

Jake rolled himself over, releasing Scott who jumped quickly to his feet and strutted naked, erect cock bouncing, over to the dresser drawer.

Jake eyed Scott's naked reflection in the full-length mirror beside the dresser, gazing at the hard, long, perfect cock as it rested on the edge of the open drawer while Scott rummaged in search of a condom and lube.

It seemed to take him forever while Jack lay propped up on his elbows, his hard-on aching for some ass. "What the hell's taking you so long?"

Suddenly, Scott turned around, condom and lube in one hand, a *Doux Baiser* chocolate in the other. "Have you ever had one of these?" He tossed the chocolate to Jake, then picked up another and popped it into his mouth. "Best chocolate in the world," he smiled, his eyelids practically melting shut at the taste of it.

Jake climbed to his feet and watched in amusement and wonder as Scott's perfect dick stiffened even more, a large jewel of pre-come sliding from the eye of his cock and spilling down his shaft as he licked the last remnants of the chocolate from his lips.

"Jesus, that chocolate must be good."

"It's almost better than sex."

"So I see," Jake said, stepping up to Scott and wrapping one strong arm around his waist. "But I think I'll be the judge of that."

Scott slammed the dresser drawer shut behind him as Jake spun them both around and onto the bed once more.

The operatic tones of another gondolier echoed from the canal below the balcony—*Nessun Dorma*, pitch perfect—as the sweat rolled down the middle of Jake's back, down the canal between his wide, clenched back muscles, his hips thrusting and cock singing inside Scott Sapphire's hard, perfect ass.

Both men's fists gripped the sheets.

Their bodies burned and throbbed and pounded.

And as Jake came inside Scott's aching body—

—as Scott came into the scrunched, sweaty sheets—

—both men cried out, their lungs heaving for air.

Suddenly, outside the balcony doors, *Nessun Dorma* stopped.

Followed by an enthusiastic cry of "*Amore per sempre!*"

With that the gondolier changed tune to his most romantic rendition of *Besame Mucho*, his voice slowly fading away along the quietly lapping canal.

"What does '*Amore per sempre*' mean?" Jake asked as Scott rolled over to face him, the two panting and shining with sweat.

"Love forever."

Jake's smile faded, his gaze becoming distant, stolen by the thoughts that raced through his head.

Scott simply smiled. "You're already in love, aren't you. With someone else."

Jake didn't answer.

Scott laughed, "It's okay. You're off the hook. My life is kind of... complicated. And romance, well it's not really on the agenda.

Besides, love can be a devil."

Jake nodded and feigned a smile. He had a different kind of devil on his mind.

His six-pack smeared with his own seed, Scott stood from the bed, leaned forward for one more kiss, and then headed for the bathroom. "Eat your chocolate. And don't disappear while I take a shower."

"I wouldn't dream of it," Jake said sitting up on the sheets, his muscular body making a dent in the bed, sheets strewn and tousled all around, covering his shins, his ankles, tossed loosely around his still hard cock.

He plucked up the chocolate that Scott had tossed to him earlier and watched Scott's bare ass make its way into the bathroom.

Scott began closing the bathroom door.

Jake popped the chocolate into his mouth. "Damn, that *is* good!"

Scott nodded knowingly. "Enjoy."

The bathroom door clicked shut.

Instantly, Jake leaped naked off the bed and headed straight for the dresser. He pulled it open and knew he'd started in the right place. Scott's credit cards and driver's license slid to the front of the drawer as he yanked it open—as well as Scott's passport.

If he was going to make it out of Italy at all, with or without the Devil of Kahna Toga in his possession—the damned diamond devil he had retrieved from the volcano of Kahna Toga, only to lose it to the depths of the Grand Canal after the collapse of Pierre Perron's *palazzo*—he was going to need the identity, and passport, of an innocent stranger.

Jake smiled, Scott's chocolate still melting in his mouth.

Unfortunately for Jake, Scott was no innocent stranger.

In the bathroom of his hotel room, Scott Sapphire walked

naked to the shower recess, casually turning on the water, before hastily backtracking across the floor and snatching up Jake's jacket, the one he had intentionally tossed into the bathroom.

Hurriedly he went through the jacket, finding what he wanted tucked in the inside left breast pocket—

—Jake Stone's invitation pass to the *Mancini Rare Treasures Lost and Loved* exhibition.

On the pass was a photo of Jake.

Scott tilted his head from one side to the other with a shrug, sizing up the picture of Jake. "I can work with that."

Outside in the bedroom, gazing into the mirror of the dresser in the hotel room, Jake looked at the photo on Scott Sapphire's passport and nodded confidently. "I can pull that off."

In the bathroom mirror, Scott practiced Jake's charming smile as he held up Jake's exhibition pass to his own reflection. He stood looking at himself, naked and cum-glistening, and said, "Hello, Jake Stone."

In the reflection of the mirror in the bedroom, Jake stood with Scott's passport held up beside to his own face, imitating Scott's photo to perfection. He grinned. "Hello, Scott Sapphire."

Suddenly, Jake blinked, his head feeling light, his knees feeling weak.

His tongue dabbed suspiciously at the chocolate on his lips before he looked in the mirror and whispered, "Oh, shit."

With that, Jake's eyes rolled back in his head.

His limbs went completely limp.

And like a hunk of steel, his unconscious body collapsed in a heap on the floor, legs buckling, knees thumping, torso crashing to the floor.

Passport still in hand.

Groggily, he opened his eyes.
He blinked and squinted.

Slowly the room came into focus, and despite the cracker of a headache, Jake sat up sharply.

He was still on the floor of the hotel room.

Still naked.

Alone.

And folded neatly on the end of the bed was a recently-pressed pink shirt.

Jake jumped to his feet.

The *Mancini Rare Treasures, Lost and Loved* exhibition was being held in the courtyard of the *Palazzo delle Prigioni*, the last known home of thousands of prisoners who crossed the Bridge of Sighs over the *Rio di Palazzo* to meet their fates.

Marco Mancini was one of the richest men in Italy. Like his now imprisoned colleague Pierre Perron, Signor Mancini enjoyed hosting lavish parties to show off his latest treasures—one of which was the recently salvaged Devil of Kahna Toga, a twelve inch tall diamond statue forged from the fires of a South Pacific volcano, an artifact that had been lost, then found, only to be lost again.

It was a relic that Mancini spared no expense in rescuing from the watery rubble and ruins beneath the Grand Canal after Perron's arrest.

It was a statue that had slipped in and out of Jake Stone's grasp so many times he had lost count.

But now he wanted it back.

Jake raced through the narrows streets, across the piazzas and over the bridges of Venice, buckling up his belt, pulling on Scott's pink shirt, tying his tie as he ran, until he arrived panting and sweating at the entrance of the *Palazzo delle Prigioni*.

Men in suits and women in stilettos stepped aside as Jake hurried up the steps and into the vestibule of the *palazzo* that led to the exhibition courtyard. Inside the vestibule was a young brunette in a black dress, clipboard in hand. She had large beautiful eyes, and diamonds to match, dripping from her ears.

"Good evening, sir," she said as Jake approached. "I'm Signor Mancini's personal assistant. My name is Elisa. Elisa Rolle."

Jake was panting, still blinking back the effects of the drugged chocolate, trying his best to compose himself. "Pleasure to meet you. I hear Signor Mancini's latest collection is somewhat impressive."

"The centerpiece is the Devil of Kahna Toga, never before exhibited in the western world."

"He must have spent a fortune to acquire it. You don't find treasures like that just sitting on the bottom of a canal in Venice."

Signora Rolle eyed Jake a little suspiciously. "No, you do not. But when you have more money than morals..." Elisa stopped herself before she said too much.

Jake smiled. "You sound like someone in the market for a new employer. My name's Jake, by the way. Jake Stone."

The Italian brunette eyed him quizzically, but not unapprovingly, before checking the list on her clipboard. "Mr. Stone, I'd like to say it's nice to meet you. But I'm afraid we've met before."

Jake looked at her, confused. "We have?"

"Yes. About twenty minutes ago."

"What do you mean?"

"Jake Stone is already here. May I please see your invitation pass."

Jake felt his jacket pockets, realizing the pass was gone. "I must have left it back at the hotel."

Mancini's assistant raised one eyebrow, amused and dubious.

Jake wiped the sweat from his brow, flustered and frantically trying to keep his hopes of stealing the Devil of Kahna Toga alive. "Okay, maybe I didn't leave it at the hotel. You see, there was this guy. He was tall and dark and handsome, and well, one thing led to another and—"

Elisa smiled and put a finger to Jake's lips to stop him. "As handsome as you are—whoever you are—I prefer to read my stories in a novel. For now though, I'm going to have to ask you to leave."

"But I—"

Jake didn't get to finish his sentence.

Suddenly, a shrill alarm sounded throughout the entire *palazzo*.

"The Devil," Jake and Elisa both uttered at the same time.

Invitations no longer mattered.

As guests rushed from the alarm, fearing a bomb, Jake and Mancini's assistant pushed their way against the tide of the exiting crowd, into the courtyard.

Elisa stopped sharply, staring at the smashed, empty display that had contained the Devil of Kahna Toga. "It's gone."

Instantly, Jake looked up. He caught sight of a figure in a suit scaling the courtyard wall and hoisting himself up onto the roof of the *palazzo* before disappearing from sight. "Not yet it isn't."

He turned and grabbed Elisa by the arm. "What's the fastest way to the roof?"

Mancini's assistant gathered herself quickly, thinking only of the precious relic. "Through those doors, up the prison stairs. It'll take you directly above the Bridge of Sighs."

Jake bolted.

He launched himself up the same stone stairs that thousands of doomed prisoners had staggered, stooped and sullen, centuries before. But there was nothing stooped and sullen about Jake's ascent. He rocketed up the steps and burst out through the roof exit, slipping on the roof tiles of the Palace of Prisoners.

Up ahead he saw the distinctly handsome silhouette of Scott Sapphire peeling off his jacket—the same jacket that Jake had peeled off him an hour before.

For a moment, Scott glanced back and saw Jake. And Jake

saw the shimmering Devil of Kahna Toga under Scott's arm.

He also saw Scott wink back at him with a smile.

"You can keep the shirt," he called. "Pink's your color."

With that he leaped off the edge of the building.

Recklessly Jake scrambled and slid down the tiles of the *palazzo*'s rooftop to see Scott land like a cat on top of the Bridge of Sighs before sprinting across it.

Without a second's hesitation, Jake jumped from the *palazzo*'s roof to the top of the bridge. He hit the side of the bridge's arched roof and grabbed desperately as his feet swung wide. He held on tight to the cornice, his legs dangling down the side of the bridge as tourists in slowly-passing gondolas below looked up and gasped.

Jake ignored them, glancing up just in time to see Scott slip the idol into a black velvet sack, sling the sack over his shoulder, and scale up the wall of the *Palazzo Ducale* to the roof above.

With a determined grunt, Jake hoisted one leg up onto the arched roof of the Bridge of Sighs before leaping onto the wall of the Ducale and pulling himself upward.

Pigeons were only just resettling on the roof after Scott's startling appearance when suddenly, one elbow, and then another, slammed against the roof tiles. The flustered pigeons took flight once more as Jake's face appeared. He coughed and spluttered as a flurry of fluffy down-feathers swirled around his face, before hoisting his legs up onto the roof.

As his feet slid on the 17th century tiles, trying to find their grip, Jake caught a glimpse of Scott disappearing over the peak of the slanted gothic roof.

He charged, dress shoes skidding, fingers pulling him along until he found his momentum. He hit the crest of the roof and saw Scott's silhouette against the vast glow of Piazza San Marco. He was headed for the rooftop of San Marco Basilica without hesitation or fear. Indeed, Scott was agile. Confident. And seemingly quite cunning. The man who had stumbled innocently into Jake's arms earlier that afternoon was now making a world class getaway that even Jake had to admire.

He didn't have time to admire things for too long though.

At that moment, Jake slipped on the peak of the rooftop and hit the tiles—*hard*— sending him into a slide down the other side of the roof.

Jake's fingers clawed and hooked at the crusty old tiles and managed to stop his slippery descent, mere feet before it could jettison him out over the *Piazzetta* where so many of history's rogues and rustlers had met their fate. Another second and Jake would have joined their ghosts. But not tonight.

He pulled himself to his feet once more and glanced toward the Basilica.

Scott had leaped across three adjoining rooftops before making one final jump onto the upper viewing balcony of the huge, multi-domed church.

Jake heard the surprised screams of tourists taking their early evening photos from the viewing balcony.

Racing for the Basilica, he jumped from one adjoining rooftop to the next before dropping down onto the Basilica's viewing balcony, scattering more stunned tourists.

He parted them quickly, muttering his apologies as he charged inside the church, through the upper level of the Basilica's artifacts displays before pushing his way down the ancient stairs and out through the doors of the Basilica—

—into the thousands-strong throng of Venetians and visitors all filling the lamp lit square of San Marco.

Suddenly, over the bobbing heads, flashing cameras, and flapping pigeons, Jake heard a commotion, a scream, a shout of abuse. Glasses smashed. He turned in the direction of the disturbance and spotted Scott bounding his way through an outdoor restaurant midway along the *Procuratie Vecchie* on the north side of the piazza.

Jake rammed his way through the crowd, heading for the restaurant.

As waiters began picking up spilled dishes and smashed glasses, and the maître d' calmed the unnerved patrons and helped them back into their seats, Jake made a less than welcome entrance by charging straight into the string quartet on the small raised platform at one end of the dining area.

Musicians and their instruments crashed over tables and sent restaurant-goers toppling and tumbling—again.

A violin bow speared a woman's spatchcock.

Another torpedoed into a bottle of French champagne, exploding the bottle and jettisoning the cork up into a lamplight which erupted in a shower of sparks.

Diners took cover. Waiters scrambled. While over it all Jake leaped from one table to the next with Scott and the stolen idol still in his sights—but only just.

Scott disappeared between the columns of the *Procuratie Vecchie*.

Jake jumped from the last table, leaving the angry, terrified screams of the outdoor restaurant behind him before charging between the columns, watching as Scott disappeared down a small side passageway, leaving only his quickly vanishing shadow along the stone wall.

Jake bolted into the passageway.

It turned left into a wider alley.

Right into a cobblestoned side street.

Which then opened out onto a canal filled with gondolas.

The normally calm waters of the Venice canal were already slapping and splashing against the stony banks on either side.

The long narrow boats were already in a state of chaos.

Gondoliers were shouting.

Passengers were shrieking.

And Scott Sapphire was leap-frogging from the bow of one gondola to the next, hopping from the precarious edge of one starboard railing to the port-side railing of the next boat.

Gondolas wobbled and twirled.

Gondolier poles smacked and whacked each other as the gondoliers swung at the bounding troublemaker who was heading toward what looked like an island of gondolas; dozens upon dozens of the slender boats were crammed together at the tourist-lined dock of *Bacino Orseolo*, Venice's most popular and crowded gondola station.

Jake glanced from the fleeing, boat-hopping thief to the nearest passing gondola—

—and jumped.

His shiny black shoes danced as he teetered on the port-side edge of the boat, his weight tipping the gondola precariously. The tourists on board rolled and screamed while the gondolier lost his balance and landed on top of his passengers.

The angry Italian flipped his straw gondolier's hat out of his face and looked up, but Jake was already making the leap to the next gondola, then the next.

The waves in the canal were getting choppier.

More and more gondolas began to pitch wildly.

Scott followed the ripple effect from one boat to the next until he began bounding his way across the island of gondolas—being abused and swiped at every step of the way—until he leaped onto the dock of *Bacino Orseolo*, scattering the crowds of frightened and flustered tourists.

He turned back to see Jake jump onto the side of a gondola at the far end of the swaying, waving island of boats. And for a moment, Jake stopped, trying to hold his balance on the edge of the gondola twenty feet away from Scott.

He glanced up to see Scott smile.

"Perhaps we'll meet again someday, Jake Stone," Scott called over the splashing waves and rolling gondolas. "Until then, *ciao bello!*"

With that, Scott put one foot on the side of the gondola nearest the dock and pushed down as hard as he could.

The gondola tipped almost to the point of capsizing before springing back the other way, knocking the gondola beside it—

—which rocked and pitched and sent the next gondola swaying violently–

—and the next—

—and the next—

—until a domino effect sent every gondola lurching, swinging and rolling outward.

Tourists clung desperately to the sides of their reeling boats.

Gondoliers tumbled into the water.

Jake saw the ripple of rocking boats come crashing toward him, but there was nowhere left to jump, no gondola left unrocked, until—

—the gondola on which Jake was already unsteadily perched was hit by the wave of calamity.

His arms spun wildly.

His legs wobbled.

His shoes slipped.

And before he knew it, Jake Stone landed with an almighty splash into the canal.

When he managed to surface amid the still swaying gondolas, coughing and gasping for air, Jake was grabbed by several hands. They seized him by his drenched jacket lapels and hauled him out of the water onto the dock. The sound of police whistles cut through the cries of the panicked passengers still clinging to their gondolas.

"That's him," someone shouted from a still-swaying gondola. "The man in the suit! He's the one who caused all this!"

Jake's sodden leather shoes squished against the stone as

he was jerked to his feet. One of the half dozen *carabinieri* now restraining him reached into Jake's jacket and pulled out his passport as Jake continued to cough up canal water, trying to get his breath. "It wasn't me. I swear it wasn't me. It was—"

"—Scott Sapphire," the officer grinned, staring at the name inside the passport. He looked up at Jake in astonishment. "Well, well, well. It seems the one night you make the mistake of carrying your *real* passport on you is the one night we carry you off to jail."

Instantly, Jake began to struggle and protest. "No wait! That's not me! I'm not him! I can explain!"

The officer laughed. "Not this time, Signore Sapphire. You've slipped through our fingers too many times before. This time, we're never letting you go."

A cell door slammed shut with a loud bang, causing Jake to drop the coins from his fingers. He bent down and gathered them up off the floor under the watchful gaze of the guard.

"Are you watching me, or are you watching my ass?" he muttered to the guard. He was annoyed and unimpressed, more with himself than anyone else. He had fallen victim to a con. He had stepped into a trap. He had been seduced.

That was normally *his* trick.

But Jake Stone had been played by a player. And now he had been reduced to making the one phone call he really didn't want to make.

"I'm entitled to one phone call," he said to the guard, who pointedly ignored him.

"Hey! One phone call." He hesitated. "Please."

Grudgingly, the guard let Jake out and walked him to a dirty payphone that was on the wall of the police station. The guard stayed close—no way was Jake going to escape on his watch.

Jake slid the coins into the slot of the payphone and dialed a number.

Someone on the other end picked up.

"Professor. It's me, Jake. I hate to tell you this, but I'm in jail. The cops think I'm some other guy. Someone by the name of Scott Sapphire."

From the other end of the line came a long, slow sigh. "Oh, dear. You know once upon a time he managed to lock Shane in a diamond vault in New York for an entire weekend. But that's a whole other story. In the meantime, I'll send Luca to get you out of there."

"Thanks, Professor," Jake said with a relieved sigh.

He was about to hang up when Maximilian Fathom said one more thing. "Oh, Jake, you didn't by chance get Mr. Sapphire's number? He's one young man I would very much like to meet some day."

"No," Jake muttered, and then hung up the phone, once more annoyed and unimpressed. He and the guard made the familiar trek back to his cell. Once inside, Jake stood for a moment, and then resignedly dropped onto the worn, thin mattress that covered the steel frame of his bed.

He couldn't help but smile to himself. "Next time you can kiss my ass, Scott Sapphire." Jake shoved his hands behind his head and rubbed his ass against the mattress. "Yeah, I think I'd like that."

Scott was dressed simply in jeans and a crisp white shirt as he made his way along Platform 2 of Venice's Santa Lucia station. He carried a single leather bag as he hurried alongside the navy blue carriages of the waiting train—the Venice Simplon-Orient-Express.

He found his carriage.

He was about to board.

Suddenly, from behind him, a customs official called. "*Scusi, signore.* May I please see your ticket."

Scott Sapphire turned and smiled. "Why, of course." He reached into the back pocket of his jeans and produced his ticket.

The customs official smiled back. "And your passport."

"It's right here," Scott replied.

He took the passport from his other back pocket and handed it to the official.

The man opened it.

His eyes moved from the photo on the passport, to the face in front of him, and back again.

Scott's expression remained calm. Smiling. Unflinching.

Slowly the official's brow creased, a little uncertain, before he said, "*Signore* Stone, would you mind stepping aside to answer a few—"

"Oh, my!" a voice suddenly gasped from behind the customs official.

The man spun about to see a young crippled woman on elbow crutches slip on the platform floor. She dropped the overnight bag she was already struggling to carry. One crutch shot out from her right forearm. She began to fall.

Scott rushed to catch her, swooping the young woman up in his arms before she hit the ground.

The customs official grabbed the sliding crutch, propping the pretty girl up as Scott lifted her, relieved and grateful, into an upright position.

"Oh, thank you! Thank you so much!" the young woman gushed, not at Scott, but at the customs official who scooped up the young woman's overnight bag as well.

"Oh, it's my pleasure," the official gushed back, his admiring gaze taking in the stylishly bobbed black hair, the pretty face, the perfect make-up. And those mesmerizing blue eyes. "May I help you aboard the train?" he asked as he handed back her crutch.

"Why yes, thank you," she replied with a smile, her accent not quite British, not quite American either.

Taking her bag for her, the customs official gently aided the young woman up the brass steps of the train. He asked to see her ticket and escorted her to her seat. And when she was comfortable, sitting by the window, her bag in the overhead compartment and her crutches by her side, the customs official smiled and said, "*Ciao.*"

And the young woman smiled and said, "*Grazie.*"

With that, the customs official alighted the train not even realizing that the man he had intended to question moments before—

—had now simply vanished.

In fact, as the train chugged out of Santa Lucia station, all the customs official could do was stand on Platform 2 and wave at the cute young woman with the black bob and the blue eyes while the Orient Express drifted slowly by.

As the train picked up speed, heading across northern Italy on its meandering journey across Europe toward Paris, the cute young woman felt the cushioned seat beneath her puff as someone plonked in the seat beside hers.

"Nice job, little sis."

Sophie Sapphire turned to see her brother, Scott, slumped quite comfortably in the seat beside her, an already opened bottle of Moet in his right hand and two champagne flutes held between the fingers of his left hand.

Sophie tried to upright the glasses as best she could as her brother began to recklessly pour. "Scott! You're spilling!"

"Then start drinking!"

He rushed one of the glasses to her lips, and with a giggle of bubbles, Sophie Sapphire took a few sips of champagne.

Out of the corner of his eye, Scott watched his younger sister and smiled. "So what's the occasion? Why the Orient Express?"

Sophie shrugged, adjusting her crippled legs with one hand

so she could settle in more comfortably, just like her handsome brother had already done. "Artie needs more time. He wants a day or so to line up the right buyers. Or should I say, *buyer*. This one's a one-man auction. Pierre Perron has bought everyone else out of the bidding. Apparently he wants the Devil of Kahna Toga back. He says it's personal. Even from prison, he's willing to do what it takes to get his treasure back. What's a few bars to a man who wants revenge?"

"Revenge? For what?"

Sophie shrugged. "Does it matter? All that matters is where the money goes."

"The Sudanese orphans, right?"

Sophie nodded and smiled. "Doing something so wrong never felt so right. It makes stealing seem almost... saintly."

Scott clinked glasses with his sister's. "You know what Artie always taught us."

Together they answered. "Never steal from the poor or polite; only ever take from the rich and arrogant, from the cruel and unkind."

Scott took another sip. "Today a diamond idol. Tomorrow... who knows."

"Actually," admitted Sophie with a knowing smile, "I know. But Artie wants to tell you the details himself. Don't worry, big brother. You're going to love it!"

Outside the window, the fields of northern Italy slowly transformed into the foothills, then mountains, of the Italian Alps as the train took the long way to Paris.

Chapter II

Paris, France

Arthur Dodge had exquisite taste. Correction—it wasn't so much exquisite as it was expensive. Exquisite taste is defined by style, a sense of grace and manner. On the other hand, expensive taste can sometimes be defined simply as an attraction to something that glitters. Like a moth to a flame. Or a shark to a shiny silver object bobbing on the surface of the sea.

Artie was neither a moth nor a shark, but oh, how he loved things that sparkled.

"Welcome to my humble abode," he said in an accent that had been swept straight off the grimy streets of London's East End. With it came a smile and the glint of Artie's diamond tooth.

"Nice place," Scott said, tossing Artie his leather bag.

Artie caught it in a panic. "Careful! What if I had dropped it?"

"With *your* fingers?" Scott smirked. "They're as sticky as a spider's web."

Artie beamed proudly. "Indeed they are. Come in, come in!"

Scott assisted Sophie in through the doors of the apartment

as Artie made a grand sweep of his arm, gesturing to the lavish living space and the concertina balcony doors opening up to a breathtaking view across Paris.

With the clunk and clatter of her elbow crutches, Sophie made her way out into the sunlight-bathed balcony. Scott and Artie joined her. "It's beautiful, Artie," she said, her eyes gazing upon the Eiffel Tower, a smile on her face.

Scott nodded.

Together, the three of them had come a long way.

Scott was only seven when he met his 'little sister' Sophie, the homeless crippled girl, in the street markets of Covent Garden where the two would sweet-talk money out of passers-by, steal chocolates and dream of being the children of rich parents. Loved. Adored. Spoiled.

But in reality, Scott and Sophie were anything but loved and adored, and especially not spoiled.

That was when Artie entered their lives, his quick hands saving them both from a dire situation.

When Artie found them, one of the first things he noticed was the children's eyes—a blue so luminous that no amount of fear or uncertainty could extinguish the hope in those wide, bright eyes. So he gave the two homeless children a surname of their own: Sapphire.

He didn't realize at the time he had given them so much more than just a family name.

He had made the three of them a *family*.

And although Scott was only a boy at the time, the homeless young orphan was already a swindler-in-training and proved to be a true protégé of Artie's more refined art of thieving.

Scott was light on his feet and quick with his hands. He was also charming, charismatic and cute, and was practically able to sweet-talk the rings off wealthy women's fingers and the watches off rich men's wrists. As the years passed by—as cute turned to handsome—chocolates turned to priceless jewels and rare treasures. Artie would line up buyers on the black market, and then write anonymous checks to various charities and nonprofit organizations around the world.

Medical research facilities.

Animal shelters.

Orphanages.

It was their way of giving something back.

Of righting wrongs.

Of balancing things out, trying to make the world a better place, somehow.

"So whaddaya think?" Artie asked now, grinning proudly as he looked out over Paris from the apartment's balcony. "Quite a find, don't you think? Just don't look down; it's something of a drop."

Naturally, Scott and Sophie both did what Artie told them not to and glanced over the edge of the balcony. Two stories below hung an unused window washer's platform rigged with pulleys connected to the base of Artie's balcony. Beyond that was a bustling street of Montparnasse.

"How long's the lease this time, Artie?"

Artie's lips curled into a sly smile. "Scotty, my boy, you know how I like to live in the moment."

"Then you should like this moment." Scott stepped forward and unzipped the bag that was still in Artie's hands before producing a bundle wrapped in cloth. He peeled away the covering and said, "Behold, the Devil of Kahna Toga."

The moment the sun hit the small diamond statue, beams of refracted light shone in all directions, almost blinding Sophie and Artie.

"Oh, my," Artie breathed, his pupils becoming tiny pinheads as he reached for the dazzling diamond statue. "It's beautiful. I can see why Pierre Perron is so willing to pay through that upturned nose of his to get it back." He took the Devil carefully in his hands. "Scotty, my lad, you've outdone yourself this time."

"Actually, I was almost completely *un*done. Apparently, I picked the wrong decoy this time. It seems we were both dealing from the same deck of cards."

Artie looked from the statue to Scott. "Well you ain't done playing aces yet, my boy. What do you think about a little trip to Monte Carlo for your next job?"

Scott was happily intrigued. "I could think of worse things."

At that moment, the front door of the apartment opened. From outside on the balcony, Artie, Scott and Sophie all looked inside to see a middle-aged man enter, keys in one hand, a suitcase in the other. It took the man a moment to look up and realize there were three strangers standing on the balcony.

Make that *his* balcony.

"Artie, did you do your homework on this place?" Scott asked.

"Of course I did. The owner's supposed to be away on business till the 14th!"

"Today *is* the 14th," Sophie told him.

"Whoops. Slight miscalculation. My mistake."

"*Qui êtes-vous la baise?*" the man screamed from inside the apartment.

"Sorry, no *Inglese*," Artie shouted back apologetically, knowing full well what the man had screamed.

"I said, who the fuck are you? And what are you doing in my apartment?" With that, the man dropped his suitcase and keys and reached for a nearby writing bureau.

"Ah, Artie," Scott said, alarm bells ringing even louder now. "Do you have an exit plan for this?"

"No," Artie answered, biting his bottom lip. "Do you?"

"I'm not the one who broke into someone else's apartment and made myself at home."

Inside, the man opened a bureau drawer and pulled out a

gun.

"Oh, shit," Scott whispered just before the first bullet smashed an ornamental urn sitting three feet away from Artie on the balcony.

Artie squealed.

Scott glanced over the edge of the balcony at the drop below, and then with one sweep of his arm, he tipped Artie backward—

—straight over the balcony railing.

Artie's legs flew up in the air just before he disappeared, his screech filling the air until—

THUNK!

Scott looked down to see Artie wide-eyed and flat on his back on the window-washer's platform, the diamond idol clutched to his chest.

"Am I dead?" Artie shouted up at Scott.

"Not yet!"

Another bullet shattered a balcony cornerstone next to Sophie. She screamed before Scott swooped her up in his arms and swung her over the ledge.

Sophie dropped her elbow crutches which clattered onto the window washer's platform below her.

Behind Scott and Sophie, the owner of the apartment came charging toward the open balcony doors, still shouting, still shooting.

"Incoming!" Scott shouted down to Artie.

With his sister in his arms, he took three steps back then made a running jump over the balcony railing.

A bullet nicked the collar of his shirt as he and Sophie fell out of sight, plunging the two stories to the platform below and landing with a thud that rattled the pulley wires.

Above them, the furious face of the owner of the apartment appeared, glaring down at them. He aimed and fired.

A bullet ricocheted off the metal platform.

"Hold on tight," Scott said.

Sophie wrapped her arms around his shoulders while Scott clung to her with one hand, using his other hand to seize the release lever and crank it hard.

Suddenly, the entire platform plummeted toward the ground.

Artie howled, squeezing the Devil of Kahna Toga tight.

Sophie held her breath.

The owner of the apartment disappeared far above them while the pavement below raced toward them.

At the last second, Scott yanked the lever back till the safety catch clicked, like jerking on an emergency brake.

The free-falling platform rocked to a halt four feet above the ground, sending stunned pedestrians running.

With Sophie still in his arms Scott hoisted himself over the railing of the platform and leaped to the pavement.

Dizzy and gasping for air, Artie grabbed Sophie's crutches with one hand and slid the diamond idol under his jacket with the other before rolling under the railing and dropping to the ground ass-first. "Bloody hell, Scotty! What are you tryin' to do, kill me?"

"I think you're capable of doing that all on your own! Did you have to pick a place with a gun in it?"

"How was I to know!" Artie shrugged innocently before smiling proudly. "Besides, you gotta admit though—pucker views, huh?" Scott rolled his eyes and hauled Artie to his feet. "Come on. Time to disappear."

In the darkness, water trickled down mossy brick walls. A train rumbled through the network of tunnels nearby, causing the ground to shake. It was followed by the sound of a cord bring pulled. A motor starting.

An old generator.

And then there was light.

They were deep inside a long-abandoned Metro tunnel.

Their metro tunnel.

With hundreds of miles of tracks criss-crossing their way through Paris' underground transport system, it was inevitable that over the years some sections would become unused, some turned into dead ends, while some entire tunnels would be deemed obsolete.

Beyond repair.

No longer needed.

No longer able to serve any suitable function to a thriving metropolis.

The same attitude that many held for the homeless.

Which is why the homeless so often found themselves so at home in tunnels just like this one in Paris.

But for Scott, Sophie, and Artie, this particular abandoned Metro tunnel under the busy streets of Montparnasse wasn't the only place they called home. They had a second home in an old abandoned Tube station between Embankment and the walls of the Thames in London. And a third under Hell's Kitchen in New York, in a service tunnel that once jutted off from the Eighth Ave subway line before half of it collapsed in 1967.

As the generator powered up, five lights scattered around the tunnel—all odd lamps with eclectic lampshades—came to life, illuminating the furniture that had been collected over the years: a red velvet sofa, a hatstand sprouting berets and fedoras, several bookcases stacked with volumes of encyclopedias and bound maps, and a large wooden desk upon which sat three computer monitors, all of which powered up when the lights kicked in. There were also curtains strung up around the place to section off the three antique beds that sat in three different corners of the tunnel's space, and another curtain that sectioned off an old army-issue shower, the kind with a tank suspended above it and a cord to release the water. One of the city's water supply pipes had been re-routed across the ceiling of the tunnel to feed directly into the tank.

Like their makeshift dwellings in New York and London, this dead-end Paris tunnel was more than just moth-eaten shabby chic. It was—

"Home sweet home," Scott said with a happy smile.

He flopped down on the sofa while Artie took the Devil of Kahna Toga out from under his jacket and placed it admiringly on the table beside the computer monitors, blue light reflecting through the facets of the diamond idol.

"Just how much is that little Devil worth to Monsieur Perron, anyway?" Scott asked, relaxing back with his hands behind his head.

"Enough for us to pay for a well in every village in Mali," Artie answered. "And buy you a new tuxedo decent enough to get you through the door of *Mer de l'Hotel D'or* in Monaco."

"So tell me the interruption-free version of why I'm going to Monte Carlo. The one *without* the part where a man whose place we broke into starts shooting at us."

"Come on, Scotty," Artie warmed. "You love those glimpses of the high life as much as I do."

"High life, yes. Afterlife, no."

"Boys, boys, boys," Sophie said, settling herself into a roller-chair in front of the three computer screens. "Shall we get down to the plot, or what?"

As soon as Sophie eased into the chair, she began sliding from one end of the table to the other, bringing up different information on each screen.

Scott got up from the sofa, quietly proud of Sophie's command of the computers. "My sis, the gadget wiz," was all he gave her.

"Are you calling me a nerd?"

"Not at all. Well, just a little."

"Well, maybe you want to listen to what this nerd has to say if you want to keep your ass out of trouble."

Sophie tapped at the keys of one computer and brought up a floor plan of a 12-story building. "These are the security files of *Mer de l'Hotel D'or*."

"You hack into security files and wonder why I call you a nerd?" Scott smirked.

"I said shut up and listen." Sophie clicked on a large room on the first story of the floor plan and a screen full of CCTV images appeared. "Still shots of the hotel's casino. These were taken last night." She clicked on one image in particular. "See the gentleman at the roulette table? That's Oscar Hudson. Founder of Hudson Pharmaceuticals and one of the richest men on the planet. The young woman next to him is—"

"Don't tell me, his trophy wife."

"Close but no. She's his trophy daughter, Ella Hudson. 2IC of the company. Together, they make quite a formidable pair. Wealthy, shrewd and powerful. But not without their flaws."

Sophie slid her chair across the floor and opened a screen on the next computer. A medical profile. "Oscar Hudson has what's called dyscalculia. It's similar to dyslexia, but instead of affecting someone's ability to form or comprehend words, it affects their number skills."

"Wait a minute," Scott interrupted. "You're telling me that one of the richest men in the world can't count?"

"He hasn't always had the condition. A recent accident impacted the intraparietal sulcus in his parietal lobe."

"Nerd," Scott said under his breath.

Sophie simply rolled her eyes and continued. "It's one of the reasons he keeps his daughter so close, but it doesn't affect his decision-making or business skills in general. However, he has managed to memorize a single sequence of numbers."

Sophie referred back to the still shot of the roulette game. "Notice the bets he's placed." She pointed to the numbers on the board with chips stacked on top of them.

Scott Sapphire and the Emerald Orchid

"Nine, eleven, nineteen," Scott observed.

"We believe it's the only sequence of numbers he can remember."

Scott shrugged. "So he bets the same numbers every night. I don't get where you're going with this."

"Rich men have safes," Sophie smiled.

Scott smiled back. "Now you're talking. You want me to steal whatever's inside Oscar Hudson's safe?"

"No," Artie answered. "At least not yet."

Sophie pulled up a third screen to reveal on old photograph of a jeweled egg. A golden egg. Laced with diamonds and pearls and propped on a small silver stand.

"This is the Golden Egg of the Romanovs. It was recently discovered in a small village in Uzbekistan and promptly acquired by Oscar Hudson.

"It must be worth a fortune."

"It is," Artie said. "But not as much as the item Oscar Hudson intends to acquire in *exchange* for the egg."

"Which is?"

Sophie clicked on another screen. "A map," she answered. "A map that will lead us to the Emerald Orchid, located somewhere in the heart of the Amazon."

With another tap on the keyboard she opened another image—an ink sketch of an open temple covered in vines and wild orchids. The stone columns of the temple were carved in the shape of giant snakes. Several natives were depicted kneeling inside the temple's antechamber, as though praying to an object in the center of the temple: a statue of an orchid—an emerald orchid—perhaps eight inches tall, sitting atop a serpent pillar.

"Legend has it," Artie continued, "that the Qixoto tribe of the Amazonas created the orchid from a giant emerald in honor of the rare Qixoto orchid, a bright green flower used to heighten the senses in many of their tribal rituals. They built the Temple of the

Orchid to house the statue and carved giant anacondas to guard and protect their precious orchids. These sketches were drawn by the botanist and explorer Dr. Benicio Rosso, reportedly the only man to ever find the temple. He also drew a map—a map that has been lost for almost a century. It's now in the possession of a woman named Tatyana Romanov, a distant descendant of Czar Nicholas II."

Scott put the pieces together. "So now Tatyana Romanov wants the egg, and Oscar Hudson wants the map. But why?"

"He wants the orchids," Sophie answered. "According to the stories, if they're true, the orchids have the potential to do almost anything. Aphrodisiac, anti-depressant, all-round remedy for just about any ailment, and one of the most powerful hallucinogenics in the world. It's a drug manufacturer's dream."

"Oscar and Tatyana are meeting tomorrow night at *Mer de l'Hotel D'or*," Artie continued, "after which, they'll board Oscar Hudson's ship to make the exchange. That's where the safe containing the egg is. We need you to wait until they board the ship and make the exchange, and then break in and steal that map as soon as it goes into the safe. We want to get to that Emerald Orchid before Oscar Hudson does."

"And steal it from the Qixoto people? Isn't it rightfully theirs?"

"The Qixoto vanished long ago," Artie said. "Nobody has seen or heard from them in decades. The Emerald Orchid belongs to the rainforest now. It's nobody's. It's there for the taking."

"Wherever *there* is," Sophie added.

Scott took a long, deep breath. "I guess I'm about to find out."

Chapter III

Monte Carlo, Monaco

The stars were diamonds.

If he could have plucked them from the sky, he would have. But Scott knew the night, and he knew she was as cunning and clever as he. There was no place on Earth he could have hidden those diamonds without the night knowing. So instead, he blew her a kiss from the hotel terrace of *Mer de l'Hotel D'or*, hanging high over the water of the Mediterannean as the waves washed against the rocks below and a warm summer breeze blew in from sea.

He stepped back into his suite and inhaled deeply.

He loved the smell of hotel rooms.

Clean linen, snapped tight.

Bubbles liberated from a popped champagne bottle.

The sweet smell of fresh come and the sweat of love-making.

A naked man on the bed.

Scott smiled, twisting his silver cufflinks into his cuffs.

He tied his bow tie perfectly in the mirror.

He slid on his dinner jacket.

He finished the glass of 1995 *Bollinger Cote Aux Enfants* champagne that he had ordered from room service, served in a chilled ice bucket on a silver tray now resting on the bedside table, accompanied by three *Pierre Marcolini* chocolates which he would save for his return from Oscar Hudson's ship, with map in hand.

"You're beautiful," said the young man lying stomach-down on the bed, his perfect round ass bare and beautiful on a nest of ruffled sheets. His accent was distinctly French, his chin resting on his crossed arms, his eyes watching Scott as he polished off his glass.

"So is this champagne. Please, finish it for me. I hate to see a good bottle go to waste." Scott sat on the bed next to the naked young man and kissed him, the sweet taste of champagne mixing with the irresistible flavor of a handsome man.

Mid-kiss, the young Frenchman rolled over on the sheets, his spent cock becoming hard once more, extending up his already glistening, cum-spilled belly. "Will I see you again?"

"No." Scott shook his head. "It's one of the things I do best."

"What's that?" the young man said.

"Disappear." Scott smiled.

The young Frenchman sighed, disappointed that their three-hour fling couldn't have lasted a little longer, yet he smiled nonetheless, knowing if nothing else he'd been left with one perfect, romantic memory. He reached for the bottle of champagne in the ice bucket by the bed and poured a glass as Scott headed for the door. At the last moment, the Frenchman eyed the chocolates on the silver tray. "My name's Sebastien, by the way. You don't mind if I eat the chocolates, too? I'm starving. Sex always makes me—"

Scott turned in the open doorway, one eyebrow raised, lips curled in a confident grin. "Touch the chocolates, and I'll kill you."

The young Frenchman froze, a chocolate already in hand, and laughed nervously. "You're joking, right?"

Scott gave a casual shrug. "Not really. It *is* chocolate, after all."
And with that he left the suite.
Smiling still.

The elevator pinged, and Scott's handsome mirror image in the silver doors parted to reveal the chaos and commotion, the decadence and delight, the extraordinary wealth and wanton waste that gave the *Mer de l'Hotel D'or* Casino its reputation as being Monte Carlo's favorite billionaire's playground.

Under the dazzling lights of the casino's three-story high ceiling, hundreds of people clustered around dozens upon dozens of tables, laughing, shouting, cheering. Gorgeous young women in low-cut gowns draped themselves over cigar-smoking men on winning streaks, blowing good luck onto fistfuls of die before they were cast.

Scott watched, his glimmering blue eyes lighting up in the shimmery reflection of million dollar diamonds and perfect strands of pearls dripping from the slender necks and gossip-hungry ears of every female in the room. Occasionally, he glanced up at the CCTV cameras concealed inside several small black orbs suspended from the ceiling, knowing that Sophie would have tapped into the live feed by now as she and Artie watched his every move.

Meanwhile, all around him, Scott heard calls from croupiers and roars of rapture or anger from gamblers.

"*Snake eyes!*"

"*Aces up!*"

"*The gentleman folds!*"

"*Dealer burns!*"

"*Full house of court cards wins!*"

As he made his way through the crowd, Scott lifted a glass of champagne from a passing waiter, his fingers like air, the steal so swift and delicate the waiter didn't even notice a glass was gone until he delivered the order to a nearby blackjack table.

Across the room, Scott spotted Oscar Hudson seated at a roulette table crowded with spectators. Opposite Oscar was a woman in her late fifties, immaculately dressed, beautiful, graceful, almost regal. Scott could only guess he was looking at Tatyana Romanov. The two had made their initial rendezvous.

He turned toward the table.

That's when the long arms of a tall, beautiful brunette wrapped themselves around his shoulders like the limbs of a spider pulling him into a kiss. She was in her late twenties, glamorous and stunning and she knew it, with a neckline on her red silk dress that plunged all the way to her diamond-studded belly button. When she was done kissing him, her shining red lips smiled seductively, and Scott instantly recognized her: Ella Hudson.

"I don't know who you are," she said, "but I just had to lay my lips on the most handsome man in the room. Tell me, are you here to sin—or score?"

"Judging by the naked man I just left in my hotel suite, I'd say I've already managed both."

Ella gave him a wicked smirk. "Care for a threesome?"

"Thanks, but although you seem extremely stylish, you're not quite my style."

"Well if I can't get you into bed, can I at least get your name?"

"Scott. Scott Sapphire."

"With eyes like those, that's a name that's hard to forget." At that point, Ella's own eyes narrowed with intrigue. "I can't pick your accent."

"It's somewhat... Transatlantic."

"Ella Hudson. Pleased to meet you."

"Likewise." This time, it was Scott's eyes that narrowed with intrigue. "Any relation to Oscar Hudson?"

"He's my father." Ella nodded over to the roulette table, and then sighed. "I'm supposed to be the heiress to his fortune, although tonight I suspect that fortune is going to be worth a little less than it was this morning. The chips are down, I'm afraid."

"How much?"

"You don't want to know." Ella nodded this time to Tatyana Romanov just as the dealer at the table rolled the ball into the spinning wheel. "He's playing roulette against a Russian. Not a wise move."

"Who is she?"

"Tatyana Romanov. A business acquaintance. One with admirable taste in men, I might add."

"Why do you say that?"

As if to answer his question, a spectator stepped aside to reveal the handsome young blond sitting beside Ms. Romanov. He was Scott's age, perhaps slightly younger. Tanned. Brown-eyed. With the kind of clean-cut American look that Scott could spot a mile away.

Yes, Scott had a weakness or two.

Ella noticed it in his eyes. "Stop staring like that. You're making me jealous."

"Who is he?"

Ella shrugged. "I have no idea."

At that moment, the roulette ball bounced to a halt. The crowd of spectators cheered as Tatyana Romanov smiled elegantly and let her blond friend plant a congratulatory kiss on her cheek. At the same time, Oscar Hudson shrugged with a good-natured grin.

"Poor Daddy," Ella said, realizing another loss at the table. "He blames Lady Unluck, more commonly known as wife number thirteen. Unfortunately, she knocked him unconscious with her jewelry box the night of their honeymoon after she discovered he'd re-kindled his flame for wife number eight. He says the blow knocked his lucky gambler's streak out of him."

"Must have been a heavy jewelry box."

"Again, you don't want to know." Ella seemed suddenly struck by an idea that enticed her. "Would you like to meet him?"

"Would you like to introduce me?"

"If it'll buy me a chance to push you into a bed with Ms. Romanov's mystery blond, then absolutely yes."

Ella seized Scott's hand and snaked her way across the crowded casino floor.

Scott heard the roulette ball bounce and roll around its spinning wheel until it dropped into one of the numbered slots.

"Red twenty-three," the dealer called.

The spectators that had gathered around Tatyana Romanov applauded once again while Oscar Hudson smiled across the table from her, refusing to let his defeat dent his distinguished façade.

"Congratulations," he said graciously. "Yet again."

"Best be careful, Oscar," Tatyana replied in her silky Russian accent. "If I keep winning like this, you may have a new majority shareholder in your company. And trust me, I can be very brazen and bossy."

"Sorry, that position's already been filled," Ella said appearing behind her father. She bent low to kiss her father on the cheek, her plunging neckline catching the envious eye of every woman and the adoring gaze of every man at the table—except Scott. And the handsome blond sitting next to Tatyana. Ella intended to rectify that immediately.

"I'm Ella Hudson," she announced, reaching across the table to shake the blond's hand.

The young man took a breath to speak before Tatyana spoke for him.

"Allow me to introduce my American friend, Mr. Thomas Truman."

"Please, call me Tom." The young blond nodded, his Texan drawl unmistakable. "It's a pleasure to meet you."

"Oh, believe me, the pleasure's all mine," Ella teased. "Allow me to return the favor. Daddy, Tatyana, Mr. Truman, allow *me* to introduce Scott Sapphire."

Tom Truman smiled politely. Tatyana Romanov almost began purring. Oscar Hudson stood to shake Scott's hands.

"Mr. Sapphire. Please join us."

Oscar had already pulled out a seat at the roulette table and was sliding ten blue chips in front of Scott's place. "Let's see what you can do with that. God knows good fortune isn't exactly smiling on *me* tonight."

Scott glanced at the chips before him. "Fifty thousand dollars? That's very generous sir, thank you. But I—"

"What's the matter? You don't enjoy taking from strangers?"

Scott smiled. "Only if it involves risk."

Oscar turned to his daughter. "I like this guy." He turned back to Scott and with a friendly pat on the shoulder and said, "Then consider this a challenge. A business deal. If the ball rolls in your favor, we split the winnings."

He held his hand out and Scott shook it firmly. "Deal."

Oscar nodded to the croupier who opened the game. "Ladies and gentlemen, place your bets."

Tatyana slid half her chips onto 20 Black, the other half onto 30 Red.

Scott watched as Oscar moved a third of his chips onto 9 Red, another third onto 11 Black, and his remaining chips onto Red 19. "Mr. Sapphire, your bet."

As the croupier spun the wheel one way and sent the roulette ball spinning in the opposite direction, Scott confidently pushed all his chips onto a single number—1 Red.

As the rolling ball began to spiral downward, the croupier declared, "No more bets." All eyes watched as the ball jumped and bounced, ricocheting off the numbers of the wheel before finally slotting into one.

"Twenty Black," the croupier called. "The lady wins again."

Tatyana smiled at Tom as the croupier swept the losing chips off the table and paid the winning bet.

"Easy come, easy go," Oscar shrugged nonplussed.

"Come now, Oscar," Tatyana smiled. "Everyone knows you better than that. You hate losing. All successful men do. Nobody builds a business empire out of losing."

Oscar changed the subject before his calm composure could crumble. "Speaking of which—" he turned to Scott and shook his hand once more. "Mr. Sapphire, it was a pleasure meeting you, but if you'll excuse us, Ms. Romanov and I have some business to attend to."

"I'm sorry I couldn't win back your money."

Oscar shrugged. "You have to take it while you can."

"I always do," Scott said.

Oscar stood and turned to his daughter. "Ella, darling, is the helicopter ready?"

"It's waiting on the helipad," Ella answered.

Across the table, Tom Truman assisted Tatyana up from her chair.

"You don't mind if Tom joins us," she said to Oscar. "I'd like some company to help me celebrate once we're done." She gave Tom a suggestive look. He kissed her once more on the cheek.

"Not at all," Oscar said, slipping a five hundred euro note into the hand of the croupier, who nodded with gratitude. "After tonight, we'll both have something to celebrate."

Tatyana, Tom, and Oscar made their way across the crowded casino floor.

Before she joined them, Ella turned back to Scott. "Why do I get the feeling you and I will meet again?"

Scott shook his head. "I'm afraid I'll be gone by morning. But first, I have one small matter to address."

Ella stood close to him and grinned as her hand slid confidently between his legs. "Something tells me none of your matters are small." She planted another kiss on him, and then said, "*Adieu*, Scott Sapphire. Until next time."

With that, Ella Hudson sashayed her way toward the elevator, her red dress swishing and gliding with each stiletto-heeled step. As soon as the elevator doors closed to take the four of them to the hotel roof, Scott moved swiftly through the casino, heading in the opposite direction of the elevators.

He pushed through an emergency exit.

He charged down the concrete stairwell, taking the steps four at a time.

He pushed through a door that took him through a network of maintenance and delivery corridors, passing a housemaid with a laundry cart who watched the man in the tuxedo race past her with a polite nod and a quick "*Excusez-moi.*"

Moments later, he burst out through an exit door at the end of the corridor and raced along a deserted alley at the side of the hotel to the harbor wall.

Away from the bright lights of the hotels and the city sloping up the mountain—his path illuminated only by a million shimmering stars—Scott inched his way along a high rock wall overlooking Monte Carlo Harbor. He reached a small ledge and stopped. Below him was a sheer drop plunging all the way down to the deep harbor waters. Lining the port were countless multimillion-dollar yachts and cruisers, with the larger private ships anchored a little farther out, lit up like sparkling jewels.

It didn't take long for Scott to spot the one vessel he was looking for—the ship he'd been watching from his hotel terrace earlier that evening.

The Shaman.

Oscar Hudson's private ship.

On the roof of *Mer de l'Hotel D'or*, hotel security escorted Oscar, Ella, Tatyana, and Tom to their helicopter. While Tatyana and Tom were ushered into the back passenger seats of the chopper, Oscar took the front passenger seat while Ella, in her slender red dress, slid into the pilot's seat and began firing up the bird.

"You can fly this thing?" Tom asked from the back.

Ella glanced back. "My father taught me everything I know. You sound surprised."

"No. Just impressed."

"Never underestimate a woman," Ella winked. "Ginger Rogers was able to do everything that Fred Astaire did—dancing backward, and in high heels. Now *that's* impressive."

As the rotors whirred into motion, Ella gave the thumbs up to the security staff on the helipad, who quickly moved away from the chopper as it prepared for lift-off.

On the rock ledge above the harbor, Scott was already half-naked. He had kicked off his shoes, pulled off his socks, and stripped off his bow tie, jacket, and shirt. His smooth chest and taut stomach shone in the light of the stars.

As he began unbuckling his belt, he heard the *thump-thump-thump* of chopper blades cutting through the night. From above, Oscar Hudson's helicopter shot overhead, flying away from the casino and heading out over the harbor, straight for the luxury ship anchored off port.

Scott yanked open his belt and unzipped his trousers.

He slid them down his thick legs.

There he stood on the ledge, facing Monte Carlo Harbor in nothing but a black Speedo. He sized up the drop to the water below, then sized up the distance between the port and *The Shaman*.

He saw Hudson's helicopter already circling the small ship, preparing to land on the helipad at the rear of the luxury boat.

He took a deep breath, filling his lungs with as much air and courage as he could.

Then, after one self-assured step—toes curling around the rocky edge of the ledge—Scott Sapphire launched himself into the night and plunged into the deep, black waters of the harbor.

Ella secured the landing skids of the chopper while Oscar led Tatyana to the spacious parlor on the lower deck, with Tom trailing behind. Oscar gestured for them to make themselves at home while he fetched glasses and a bottle of Dom Perignon from the bar at the end of the parlor. The room was furnished with antiques and adorned with countless ancient artifacts encased in glass.

Tatyana took a seat on a 19th century Parisian chaise lounge, her back and shoulders instantly enveloped in its soft velvet touch. "Oscar, I must get the number of your decorator."

"Actually, that would be me," Ella said, gliding into the room as her father slid a glass of champagne into her hand.

"My, my," smiled Tatyana. "You *are* a woman of many talents. I'm expecting you to dance backward in those heels at any moment."

Ella laughed, then turned to notice Tom studying the encased artifacts on the walls.

"What is this?" Tom asked.

"It's the death mask of a medicine man from the Butu tribes of Papua New Guinea," Ella answered. She couldn't help but smile, seeing the horror dawn in Tom's eyes. "Yes, it's a man's face."

"They cut someone's face off?"

"Not just someone," Oscar explained, handing a glass of champagne to Tatyana. "That's the face of the tribe's medicine man. When he died, it was believed his power of healing was passed on to the next medicine man through his death mask. They would cut off the dead man's face and place it over his successor's face for three full moons. In that time, the new medicine man could see any illness, and any cure, through the eyes of the dead shaman. Through those eyes he could prescribe the appropriate remedy for any ailment. The root of the kahnaka plant found only on the southern side of the mountains. The hide of a vampire bat, skinned wings and all, and boiled into a scalding black soup. The lock of a warrior's hair. The eyelashes of a virgin. The teeth of a dead infant still buried deep in its gums. Some see this sort of practice as primitive. Others look at that face and see only the macabre." Oscar took a sip of his champagne and looked into the hacked-out eye sockets of the human mask beneath the glass. "Myself? I look into the face of death, and I see the history of healing. And its future."

Oscar handed Tom a glass of champagne. He took it distractedly, unable to take his eyes off the leathery swathe of human skin—its eyes, nose and mouth sockets missing—stretched and pinned beneath the glass. "Oh, thank you," he eventually managed when he realized there was a glass in his hand.

"You're welcome," Oscar said. "And please, my apologies for the lack of staff on board the ship tonight. I gave my crew the night off. So that we could have a little privacy, you understand."

"Of course," Tatyana said before turning to her young companion. "Thomas, darling. Why don't you go enjoy some fresh air on the bow of the ship while Mr. Hudson and I conduct business? We wouldn't want to bore you with our affairs."

Tom nodded obligingly. "Of course. I'll leave you to it."

His handsome face broke the surface of the water. He gasped for air, his hair as black as the cloak of night and slicked back from his forehead. He reached for the ladder that dipped into the warm Mediterranean waters off the back of the ship.

The sea water slid silently down his body as Scott climbed the ladder—his abs rippling, his wet arms and legs shining—before he stepped silently aboard the unmanned ship.

Quickly, he sized up his surroundings.

There were three decks above the waterline.

On the upper deck, Scott saw the chopper on its landing pad and the lights of the bridge shining down on the deserted bow of the ship.

On the mid-deck, several cabins were lit.

And on the lower deck—the deck on which he was standing now—internal lights illuminated the long parlor in which Oscar, Tatyana, and Ella sipped champagne and talked. The glass doors leading into the parlor were open, and as Scott pressed his wet back against the side of the ship to conceal himself, the voices of Oscar and his guests carried outside into the quiet air of the Mediterrean.

Scott caught every word.

"I trust you have the map."

"I trust you have the egg," Tatyana replied.

"Yes," Oscar said. "It's in a very safe place."

"I'd like to see it. I've been searching for this egg for a very long time."

"First, the map," Oscar demanded.

Tatyana stood from the chaise lounge, reached into her handbag and produced a small silver cylinder. She stepped forward and placed it on the table in the middle of the parlor.

Oscar placed his champagne down and slowly set his hand on the cylinder.

Tatyana quickly set her hand on his. "I'd like to see the egg. Now!"

"And I'd like to see the map."

For a moment the two stood over the cylinder before Tatyana eventually let her hand slip away.

Oscar smiled and opened the cylinder.

He played his poker face once again as he slid the ancient map from the silver tube, unraveling an ink-smeared parchment that was itself sealed in a clear, water-tight plastic sleeve. The map was covered in intricate etchings—jungle canyons, rivers, deltas, waterfalls, a web-like bridge, a temple with several symbols surrounding it. Oscar had done enough research on the map's markings and parchment to know he was looking at the genuine article.

"Ella, darling. Would you please take this to the safe in my bedroom suite? And bring Ms. Romanov her egg. But first, be so kind as to top up our glasses. I believe Tatyana and I have a deal."

Tom Truman didn't go to the bow of the ship for some fresh air as he said he would.

Instead, he made his way straight to Oscar Hudson's bedroom suite on the mid-deck, exactly where C.I.A. Intel said it would be.

As part of the Agency's Preemptive Strike Unit, Special Agent Thomas Truman had been working on Tatyana Romanov 24/7 for the better part of a week now, not in an attempt to get to the egg, but to intercept the map that she was about to hand over to Oscar Hudson. Tom had tried several times to get his hands on the key to the safety deposit box in which the map was contained, but Tatyana had kept the key well concealed before tonight's exchange.

Now, Tom had only one card left to play: hide in the master bedroom suite until Ella came to open Oscar Hudson's safe and swap the map for the egg, at which point he would pull his gun and his badge.

The master bedroom suite was large and luxurious.

There was a satin-sheeted king-sized bed set against a wall at the far end of the suite. On the starboard side was a large mahogany desk adorned with artifacts, while standing along the port side of the suite were three totem poles carved with wild animals and birds. There were large windows—not mere portholes—along the port and starboard walls of the suite with curtains draped from ceiling to floor.

Tom quickly made his way around the mahogany desk and hid behind a curtain on the starboard side of the suite. He reached into his tuxedo jacket and with his left hand pulled out his standard issue Glock 22 pistol—the one that the C.I.A. agent posing as a security guard at the entrance to the casino had conveniently overlooked. He knew he wouldn't have to wait long before someone came for the egg in the safe.

Inside the parlor, Ella opened another bottle of champagne to refill Oscar and Tatyana's glasses.

Meanwhile, outside on the deck, Scott ducked low and hurried along the port-side walkway of the vessel. Time was against him. He had to find the master bedroom suite, locate the safe and hope to hell that Sophie and Artie were right about the combination numbers. For although Scott was primarily here for the map, he wasn't about to get this close and pass up the chance to steal a golden egg as well.

Swiftly he scaled a set of steps up to the mid-deck and began weaving his way through the ship, trying every door he came upon until a pair of double doors opened up to reveal a bedroom suite so stately and lavish it had to be the master bedroom.

He stepped inside, closed the doors behind him and scanned his surroundings.

A bed.

A desk.

Three totem poles.

No paintings on the walls to conceal a safe.

Scott quickly turned toward the desk.

He began pressing the wood paneling, feeling for a trigger, a secret compartment. He felt along the lip of the surface and slid underneath the desk, still dressed only in his Speedo, looking for a concealed switch, a secret lock, anything that looked out of the ordinary. There was nothing.

Scott pulled himself out from under the desk and looked around for any other clues to the safe's whereabouts.

He stepped up to the three totem poles.

He studied the one on the right, the faces of three brightly-painted creatures stacked one on top of the other. A bear, a beaver, a raven.

He looked at the totem pole on the left. A wolf, a snake, an eagle.

His eyes settled on the totem pole in the middle.

A bear with a beaver in its mouth.

A raven with a frog in its beak.

An eagle with a snake in its talons.

Scott smiled and said to the pole. "I bet you ate the egg, too."

Hastily, his fingers began probing and prodding the pole.

He pressed against the carved face of the bear, his fingers venturing into its wide open mouth where the face of the beaver stared out from between the bear's jaws. He felt his way up to the raven and pushed against its beak. He continued upward to the snake looped in the eagle's talons.

The serpent formed a perfect circle, its tail caught in its own fangs.

Scott took hold of the snake in one hand and jiggled it.

It gave a little.

Scott grinned. This was more than just a carving.

As though he was holding onto a key in a door, Scott wriggled the circular snake until it gave way completely, sliding in a counter clockwise direction.

At the same time, he heard latches inside the totem pole unlock, and suddenly—

—the large wooden beak of the eagle sprang open to reveal a small safe inside.

Scott's fingers hastily seized the dial.

He twirled it left three complete rotations before slowing down and stopping on number nine.

He spun the dial right and stopped on eleven.

He turned it left again and stopped on nineteen.

He heard the lock inside release with a soft click.

He took the lever of the safe in his hand and pulled.

Scott let out a silent sigh of relief as the door to the safe opened, revealing the egg. The Golden Egg of the Romanovs. About the size of a goose egg. Laced with diamonds and pearls and propped on a small silver stand.

With a hand as steady as rock, Scott reached into the safe and took the egg off the carriage that cradled it.

It was dazzling.

The gold shimmered in the light.

The diamonds shone in his eyes.

The pearls twirled with tiny rainbows as he turned the egg in his hand.

And suddenly—

—the snout of a gun pressed against the back of Scott's wet, black hair.

"Don't move."

Scott froze, confused. If anyone were to sneak up behind him, he was expecting it to be Ella Hudson.

But this voice was male.

And Texan.

"Tom?"

"I said, don't move," the blond agent ordered. "I'm with the C.I.A. And you, sir, are about to screw up one very important assignment."

"The C.I.A?"

That question came not from Scott, but from Ella who had appeared behind Tom, *her* pistol now pressed into the back of Tom's blond hair.

Tom froze.

Ella cocked her weapon. "I knew you two boys were too good to be true. So are you both C.I.A.?"

"Are you kidding?" Scott laughed. "Have you seen what I'm wearing? Where the hell am I gonna hide a badge? Or a gun for that matter?"

"I don't doubt you're packing *something* in that swimsuit of yours, Mr. Sapphire." Ella smirked. "But if you hadn't noticed, you're at the front of a conga line of pistols. With a precious artifact in your hand. Which means I don't care if you're C.I.A. or not. You're not leaving this ship this alive, and neither is Agent Truman."

Scott gave a casual shrug and turned to face both Tom and Ella. "But I thought you wanted a threesome."

"I said, don't move," Tom ordered instinctively, his gun now aimed at Scott's smiling face.

"And I'm telling *you* to shut up," Ella ordered Tom. With one hand, she pressed her pistol even harder into the back of Tom's head. With her other hand, she clutched the silver cylinder even tighter, the one containing the map to the Emerald Orchid.

Scott noticed. He quickly looked Tom in the eye and shrugged apologetically. "I'm really sorry to do this, but you'll thank me later... Maybe."

"Do what?"

Scott jerked his knee as hard as he could up between Tom's legs, slamming him in the balls so hard that handsome C.I.A. agent instantly doubled over with a stunned gasp.

As he did so, Scott snatched the pistol from his hand and pointed it straight at Ella.

For a split second Scott and Ella stood facing each other— Ella with the map cylinder in one hand and her gun now aimed straight ahead at Scott; Scott with the Golden Egg in one hand and Tom's gun now aimed straight at Ella; with Tom gasping in agony on the floor between them.

But not for long.

No sooner had he hit the ground, Tom kicked one leg backward, despite the explosive pain in his balls. His shoe connected with Ella's shin, hard.

Ella's leg buckled, her ankle twisting out of her shoe as the heel snapped.

Her gun went off with a loud crack, the bullet whistling past Scott's head as he ducked.

The bullet slammed into the wing of the eagle, splintering its wooden feathers.

As Ella continued to topple backward, Scott spun about, fired Tom's gun, and shot the glass out of the window behind the totem poles.

Ella hit the floor.

She let slip the map cylinder but not her gun.

She pumped off another bullet in Scott's direction, this one clipping the Golden Egg in his hand and sending it flying out the shattered window.

Scott watched the egg disappear into the dark before glancing back to see the map cylinder roll across the floor and bump straight into Tom.

Tom snatched it up.

Scott snatched Tom and pulled him to his feet.

"Time to go."

As Ella fired off another two shots, Scott and Tom leaped through the shattered window, both of them landing with a thud on the port-side deck. As Scott hit the boards, he looked up to see the egg rolling toward the edge of the deck.

Desperately, he reached for it, but just as his fingers brushed against the jeweled treasure, he felt himself being jerked away. Tom had him by the shoulder.

Scott watched, helpless and wide-eyed, as the Golden Egg

rolled off the deck and plopped into the harbor.

As Tom yanked him to his feet, he spun Scott around. He slid the map cylinder into the inside pocket of his tuxedo jacket and grabbed the gun out of Scott's hand. "I'll take that back, thanks," he spluttered, still trying to cough his balls back into place.

Scott handed over the weapon without a struggle, smiling sympathetically at the strained look on Tom's face as he tried to take back control. "You're kinda cute, you know."

Another bullet fired at them from inside the bedroom suite.

Tom dropped and pulled Scott down onto the deck out of the path of the shot. Scott landed directly on top of him and both men grunted, the scantily clad thief pressed hard against the tuxedoed C.I.A. agent.

For a second, they stared at each other, their noses practically touching, before Tom uttered, "We gotta get to that helicopter and get the hell outta here."

"You can fly?"

"I'm C.I.A. We can do everything."

At that confident comment, Tom felt Scott's cock push hard and stiff against his crotch.

A smile flashed across Scott's face.

For the briefest of moments, Tom didn't move, enjoying the moment, before saying, "You know, when we get outta here I'm duty-bound to arrest you."

"Let's get outta here first," Scott pointed out.

As he spoke, Ella leaned out the shattered window and fired another shot that ripped a hole in the deck beside Tom's head.

Like lightning, Tom and Scott sprang to their feet.

Ella took aim again, but her weapon made a hollow click, its cartridge spent. "Fuck!" she cursed, vanishing inside.

Without wasting another second, Tom and Scott sprinted to the upper deck at the stern of the ship.

Inside the vessel, Ella limped quickly into the lower deck

parlor.

"Did I hear shooting?" Oscar Hudson turned in alarm as soon as Ella entered the room. "Where's the map?"

"And where's the egg?" Tatyana demanded urgently.

"The egg's history, and the map will be, too, if I don't get my hands on a gun!"

Oscar opened a drawer behind the bar.

He pulled out two pistols and threw one to his daughter.

Tatyana gasped, horrified not by the sight of the weapons but at the thought of her Golden Egg being lost forever.

On the helipad deck, Scott unfastened the skids while Tom strapped himself into the pilot's seat of the chopper. He flicked on the fuel boost and hit the engine switch. The propeller blades began to whir into motion.

Ella and Oscar came racing up the steps to the upper deck as guns in hand.

Scott pulled open the passenger door and scrambled inside and bullets ricocheted off the chopper's fuselage in a firework display of sparks.

"Get us up!" Scott shouted to Tom.

But Tom didn't need to be told twice. He was already gunning the throttle. With a violent shudder, the bird lurched forward and swooped recklessly into the air.

"Jesus, are you sure you can fly?"

"Shut up!" Tom shouted back, trying to get the chopper off the deck as fast as possible.

The bird veered left, tilted right, and then swung so close to the upper deck that Oscar and Ella had to drop for cover before the chopper swept clear of the ship and sped off into the night.

"Fuck!" Ella screamed again.

As the helicopter flew low over the harbor, Tom glanced at Scott. "Are you hurt at all?"

"No, I'm fine."

"Good, because as soon as we find a safe place to land you're gonna be answering a lot of questions. The first of which is: how the hell did you get that safe open back there."

Scott grinned. "I told you, I'm a thief. It's one of the two things I do best."

"What's the other?"

"Disappear."

With one hand, Scott reached into his swimsuit, his still stiff cock protruding high and hard. He gripped it in his hand and pulled it out of his snug-fitting Speedo.

Only it wasn't his cock.

It was the map cylinder.

Desperately, Tom patted his empty tuxedo pocket, realizing that Scott had snatched the cylinder when he fell on top of Tom on the deck.

"By the way, if it's any consolation," Scott said with a smile, "you really did give me a hard-on."

"Shit!" was all Tom could say, trying to make a grab for the map while keeping the bird in the air at the same time.

But Scott already had the passenger door open. "Oh, and sorry about kicking you in the balls. Maybe I could make it up to them sometime."

With a wink and the cylinder firmly clenched in his fist, Scott launched himself out of the low-flying chopper, diving into the dark harbor below.

"Goddammit!" Tom shouted, knowing the map had just slipped through his fingers.

As the chopper swept away into the night, Scott broke the surface of the black water with a smile on his face—

—and the map to the Emerald Orchid in his hand.

Chapter IV

Nice, France

"The C.I.A. was there? What do you mean the C.I.A. was there!"

"I mean the C.I.A. was there!" Scott repeated quietly over the phone to Artie. He was now dressed in jeans, a white shirt and sunglasses, leaning against a payphone booth at Nice Airport, scanning the terminal for the police, Interpol, anyone who might come looking for him.

"How many C.I.A. agents were there?" Artie asked in a mild panic.

"Calm down, Artie; it's okay. It was just the one." Scott smiled to himself as he added, "And he was cute, too."

"Scott, keep your mind on the job!"

"I can multitask, can't I?"

"Just concentrate on multitasking your arse to Manaus. You need to find Dr. Osvaldo Torres. He's a botanist and an expert in the works of Dr. Rosso. He may be the only one who can make sense of the map." Artie paused for a second. "You do have the map, don't you?"

Scott patted the crotch of his jeans. "It's somewhere safe," he answered. He figured keeping the map stashed inside his briefs was as good a place as any, although he had long discarded the silver cylinder in favor of passing through airport security undetected. "And I almost had the Golden Egg, too!"

"One thing at a time," Artie said. "The egg can wait."

"Right now, it's waiting at the bottom of the Mediterranean."

"It'll turn up again someday; don't worry about it. Focus on one thing at a time, would you... and I don't mean the cute C.I.A. agent! Scott, you have to find the Temple of the Orchid before anyone else does."

"It's okay, Artie, I'm focused. Monte Carlo taught me one thing, that's for sure."

"What's that?"

"Oscar Hudson wants that map."

Chapter V

Rio de Janeiro, Brazil

"I want that map!" Oscar Hudson roared, slamming his fist on the twenty-foot marble table in the dining room of his Rio mansion.

After Tom Truman and Scott Sapphire had taken off from the boat in Oscar's helicopter, Oscar and his daughter knew they had to get out of Monte Carlo—fast!

Gun in hand, Oscar thanked a frantic and furious Tatyana Romanov for her time before promptly throwing her overboard, a distraction for the local water police while Ella and Oscar hauled up anchor and steered *The Shaman* at full speed to Genoa, Italy, where Oscar had summoned his private jet to take them to his mansion in Rio as quickly as possible.

The mansion itself was set into the sheer cliff face of *Morro da Urca*, the sister peak of Sugarloaf Mountain, overlooking the yacht-filled Guanabara Bay. A polished concrete and glass structure designed by one of New York's finest architects, the house jutted out from the cliff-face overlooking a drop of 600 feet. One hundred feet above the exclusive residence were the cable car stations running visitors all the way to the top of Sugarloaf Mountain. The only access to the mansion was via helicopter (fortunately, the one stolen in Monte Carlo was not the only chopper in the Hudson empire), one of which now sat on the helipad of the mansion's flat-topped roof beside a fifty-foot-long infinity pool.

Inside the mansion, Oscar stormed away from the marble dining table and stood at the floor-to-ceiling glass wall that overlooked the bay and all of Rio, staring out over the city's crystal waters and white sandy beaches, its clusters of apartment buildings and hotel towers and tiny sardine-packed slums rising up into the mountains, while Christ the Redeemer with his arms outstretched stood atop Corcovado Mountain watching over the tightly-packed metropolis.

Behind him, Ella took a glass of champagne from a tray carried by Oscar's ever-loyal houseboy Leandro—a handsome, green-eyed, twenty-four-year-old Brazilian hired to serve drinks; to clean the pool; to keep Oscar's wives distracted when they caused him grief; and to take care of any 'problem matters' that should arise. After all, Oscar Hudson was a man of great wealth, and with a lot of money came a lot of enemies.

Leandro offered a glass to Oscar as well, but the enraged billionaire struck the silver tray from Leandro's hands.

The tray clanged, and the glass smashed on the slick marble floor.

"The Qixoto orchid could potentially be the greatest designer-drug this planet has ever known," Oscar shouted at Ella and Leandro. "Don't you understand? The healing properties of the drug combined with its hallucinogenic components could make it the most addictive, legalized drug in history. Everyone from cancer patients to rock stars will be hooked. With this orchid, we could rule the world. I want that map! I *need* that map!"

"No, you don't," Ella said with a sip of champagne. Her tone was not so much defiant as it was confident. "It's not the map you need, it's the orchids. My guess is that the sly and sexy Mr. Sapphire has given the C.I.A. the slip and is already making tracks to follow the map. Let him do all the hard work. Then, all we have to do is follow him. Leave this one to Leandro and I. We'll find your orchids."

Ella glanced at Leandro, who smiled back, silently thrilled by the thought of solving another 'problem matter'.

At the same time, Oscar turned to his daughter.

The rage slowly drained from his face, and a smile appeared.

He stepped forward and brushed her hair, his tone suddenly contented, tender, perhaps even more. "You see? This is why I need you by my side." He took her glass of champagne and toasted, "To us."

Oscar swallowed a gulp of Ella's champagne first before she took back her glass.

"To us," she said, and finished off the glass—

—before planting her mouth on her father's lips.

Chapter VI

Manaus, Brazil

In the remote heart of the Amazon, the city of Manaus rises from the dense sprawl of the rainforest like an island; a bustling hub of trade, rich in culture and history. The city's inhabitants love and admire their rainforest, as well as the two rivers—the Amazon and the Rio Negro—that join to form one river near the city's southern ports. They revere their rivers, they respect the jungle, and they appreciate its bountiful food.

Cecilia Sanchez was no exception.

She was a buxom woman with a big heart and an appetite to match.

Unfortunately, according to her doctor, even the biggest of hearts are prone to attacks. It was the third time he had tried to put her on a diet and, as he so succinctly put it, his last attempt to save her life.

But Cecilia loved her food far too much to give it up, so in order to lose a few pounds, she decided to exercise harder rather than eat less. Doctor's advice was one thing, but Cecilia wasn't about to stop enjoying the tender meats and exotic delicacies the Amazon offered. She had grown up on the popular alligator meats of the region and would much rather work up a little sweat than give up her soupy *tacaca* and *picadinho de jacare*.

And so it was that the full-bosomed forty-year-old's weight-loss regime was less about resisting the calories and more about bouncing and jumping and thumping around her small fourth-story apartment to her favorite, frenzied Latin beats, turned up to full volume in an effort to exercise the fat off.

The walls of her apartment would vibrate.

The floors would shudder.

And every now and then, the alarm of a car out on the humid streets of the Amazonas capital would start blaring as a result of the ear-rupturing rumba beats thundering out through the open balcony doors of Cecilia's little apartment.

Unfortunately, for the neighbors, the walls of the apartment building were thin.

The old man in the apartment to the right of Cecilia didn't care so much on account of the fact that he was ninety-eight years old and deaf as a post.

But for the neighbor on the other side, retired botanist Dr. Osvaldo Torres, the noise would sometimes become unbearable.

On this particular day, as Osvaldo scanned through several maps of the Amazon and took countless text books down from his well-stocked bookshelf in preparation for the arrival of his guest, he heard Cecilia arrive home from her daily trip to the grocery store and braced himself for the floor-pounding music.

Sure enough it began, and with all his patience, the once-renowned professor simply gritted his teeth and continued to pore over his papers. He rehearsed in his head the embarrassing apologies he would be making to his guest, a young man by the name of Scott Sapphire who had called to arrange a meeting regarding Dr. Benicio Rosso and the legendary Qixoto orchid.

Osvaldo hadn't been asked about the orchid for a very long

time.

He was thrilled by the thought that somebody was interested in the flower, and anxious to know why. Could his visitor have some information that might lead to the orchid?

Osvaldo tried to contain his excitement.

In the meantime, the walls began to vibrate, as they always did.

The floor shuddered, more from the thudding weight of Cecilia's frantic footwork than the actual Latino beat.

Suddenly, out of time with the music, there was a loud bang on the floorboards... which stopped shuddering altogether.

As the music continued, it crossed Osvaldo's mind that perhaps his weight-challenged neighbor had suffered a heart attack in mid-step. He got up from his chair and began heading for the door, when the music ceased as well.

She must be all right, he thought to himself. *She's turned the music off. Perhaps she slipped, and then decided she'd had enough. Thank Christ for tha*t!

He didn't give it another thought, for at that moment there came a knock at the door.

"Dr. Torres?" the young man asked as Osvaldo opened the door.

"You must be Mr. Sapphire. Please come in."

"You can call me Scott," Scott said with a handshake, stepping into the apartment.

"And you may call me Osvaldo," Dr. Torres replied, leading Scott to his desk. "Come, come, I've been sorting through everything I have on Dr. Rosso and the Qixoto. I have books and charts and illustrations. The one thing I don't have—"

"—is this," Scott finished for him.

He placed the map on the desk in front of Osvaldo, whose eyes instantly lit up. "Is this what I think it is?"

Scott nodded.

Osvaldo looked from the map to Scott and back again, his mouth agape. "But where? Where did you find it?"

"It's a long story, one I don't really have time to explain. There are other people, not so nice people, who want to get their hands on it."

Osvaldo quickly put two and two together. "They want the orchid, don't they? They want to harvest it, don't they, and in the process they'll destroy its natural habitat. Every day, more and more of our rainforest vanishes. One species after another is becoming extinct. You mustn't let anyone with the wrong intentions find those orchids."

"I don't plan to."

Osvaldo eyed Scott curiously. "Then forgive me for asking, but what exactly is *your* intention? Why do you have the map in the first place?"

Scott paused a moment. He knew he could not lie to this passionate, kind old man, so instead he did a little negotiating with the truth. "There's an emerald orchid," he said.

Osvaldo nodded. "Yes, inside the temple that Dr. Rosso found."

"What if I told you that that emerald has the power to save the rainforest, to protect the surroundings that have kept it hidden and safe for so long?"

"You want to steal the emerald?"

"Not steal it. I want to use it. For the right reasons."

"Your motivations seem... dubious... Mr. Sapphire. You want to steal a native treasure and sell it?"

"And dedicate the money to conserving the Amazon." Scott nodded.

"But the Emerald Orchid belongs in a museum. Better yet, it belongs where it is right now, where the Qixoto intended it to be."

"Tell me, Dr. Torres... Osvaldo... what good is an emerald in the middle of a rainforest that may not be there for much longer?

That temple won't stay lost forever. Would you rather I find it? Or a bulldozer? If the emerald was created to help protect the orchid, then let it do exactly that."

Osvaldo sighed. "So it would seem I must lose a battle to win the war. Very well," he said reluctantly. "Pull up a chair." He picked up an old journal with a leather-bound cover. He blew the dust off it. "This is Rosso's original diary. He was a man devoted to his science. A true believer in the beauty and healing powers of plants. In the end, he died of malaria after contracting the parasite on his final expedition, although nobody knew. As the fever took hold, it drove him insane, and people began believing he was nothing more than another mad scientist. He began talking to his specimens. He trusted them more than he trusted his fellow man, a view he made public in several paranoid—yet well-documented—incidents. He ostracized himself, and soon his colleagues joined his rivals, and the whole world turned against him. They mistook his research as the rantings of a lunatic. Some of his work was destroyed; many of his books and writings were lost forever. And this map of yours simply vanished."

Osvaldo pulled a pair of amber-rimmed reading glasses out of his shirt pocket and unfolded a large chart of Amazonas region west of Manaus.

"Manaus is here," he said, pointing. "It's the junction where the Amazon River meets the Rio Negro—the Black River. In 1936 Rosso journeyed along the Amazon, past the town of Manacapuru until he came to *Lago Acarituba*, about a hundred miles southwest of here."

He turned the pages of the diary, turning carefully past illustrations and notes, and found an entry dated March 11, 1936. "The Black River is rising, the annual flooding is about to begin. We have journeyed as quickly as possible to *Lago Acarituba*. The tributaries and *igapo* surrounding the lake are a labyrinth, a tangle of waterways. I fear we may never find the orchid, or find our way out. I will draw a map and keep it safe."

"What's an *igapo*?"

"The swamps of the Amazon rainforest. Very dangerous places."

Osvaldo took Rosso's original map gently in his hand—smiling at the detail, cherishing the sight of a parchment he had always believed was gone forever—and slid it over the Amazonas chart. "Here is *Lago Acarituba*," he pointed on the chart. "And here it is on Rosso's map. Three tributaries in a row on the left bank of the Amazon, the third leading to the lake. Then through the *igapo* to Diabo Falls and beyond."

Both Scott and Osvaldo followed the old man's finger along a line on the map, heading south of the lake, through a maze-like network of small streams and swamps, past the drawing of a waterfall and the web-like bridge—

—to the depiction of a temple.

"You really will be entering the unknown," Osvaldo warned.

Scott pointed to several spiral swirls drawn on the map around the temple. "What are these?"

"That's the Qixoto symbol for anaconda. The guardians of the orchid." Osvaldo took his glasses off and looked Scott in the eye. "The one thing more powerful than the Qixoto Orchid is the rainforest that wants to keep its secret."

Leandro's green iris brightened with the light that streamed through the peephole. He pressed himself silently against the back of the apartment door, his brow shiny with sweat.

Through the peephole, the convex, hall-of-mirrors figure of a man walked along the corridor outside and passed in front of the door, filling the peephole as he walked by.

Leandro instantly recognized Scott Sapphire from the CCTV images that Ella had bribed out of the *Mer de l'Hotel D'or* casino security staff.

Leandro listened now as Scott's footsteps reached the end of the hall and descended the stairs of the apartment building. He took a small pouch out of his pocket and sat down at Cecilia Sanchez's dining table. He opened the pouch and took out his tobacco, his paper, his lighter, and patiently he rolled a cigarette.

He flicked his cigarette lighter and sat there smoking, blowing thin blue rings into the air.

When he was finished—when he was certain Scott Sapphire was long gone—Leandro replaced his pouch and glanced at the lifeless body of Cecilia Sanchez lying on the floor behind him.

Cecilia's legs were twisted and tangled, never to bounce or jump or thump again. Her dead eyes were staring under the sofa, as though she were shocked to find something hidden there. Her tongue bulged in her mouth and her face was already turning blue. Forgetting his strength as he sometimes did in moments of sheer exhilaration, Leandro had pivoted Cecilia's head so hard and fast that inside her throat, the broken bones of her neck were now pushing against the fat under her chin and had caused a large purple lump to form there. It looked as though she had choked on her own snapped vertebrae.

Leandro exited the apartment, silently closing the door behind him. He walked quietly to the next apartment, that of Dr. Osvaldo Torres.

He took something else out of his pocket.

A switchblade.

He held it down low and knocked gently on the door.

Osvaldo asked who was there, but opened the door before anyone answered, thinking that perhaps Scott had forgotten something and returned.

At first, the old man didn't think anything was wrong when he saw the stranger standing in front of him. It was Leandro's smile that gave it away.

His teeth were shimmering and white.

His grin handsome and wide.

Yet it was the coldest smile Osvaldo had ever seen.

And the last.

As the sun sank in the sky, Leandro left the apartment building and walked to the corner where the black Porsche was waiting. He slid into the passenger seat.

"Don't get blood on the leather," Ella warned from behind the wheel, sunglasses on.

"Your father pays me well to clean up his problems. Which means I'm more than capable of cleaning up after myself."

Ella smiled. "You've still got a little more scrubbing to do. While you were busy taking care of the good doctor, I stopped by Mr. Sapphire's hotel and spoke with the concierge. A tip in exchange for a tip off. Mr. Sapphire has chartered a boat to journey down the Amazon first thing in the morning. I think we should make sure the tour operator gets a good night's sleep, don't you?"

A wide grin spread across Leandro's handsome face.

Ella started the engine of the Porsche with a roar.

Chapter VII

The Amazon River, Brazil

The sun rose and turned the junction of the Black River and the Amazon into liquid gold. Scott had found his way to the southern ports of Manaus and was now walking toward the end of a long pier. Here, he was only a few minutes' cab ride from the center of the city, and yet already he felt a million miles from civilization. Below him, the hungry and unpredictable waters of the Rio Negro lapped at the pier's pylons. All around, he heard the caws and chirps and cries of the rainforest's inhabitants heralding a new day.

Then, he heard another sound.

It was the *chug-chug-chug* of a struggling motor.

An old riverboat, seemingly handmade, was puttering through the water, heading toward the pier. As Scott reached the end of the jetty, the riverboat's engine died down, and the boat drifted toward a rendezvous with the pier.

A young man emerged from a small makeshift cockpit cabin at the stern of the boat.

He was muscular and handsome, wearing nothing but cargo

shorts and a tight singlet with a map of fresh sweat stains down the chest. He smiled at Scott and called "*Ola*," before picking up a coiled rope and jumping from boat to dock with confidence.

He reined the riverboat in and secured it to the pier before shaking Scott's hand. "Mr. Sapphire, I presume?"

Scott nodded. "Call me Scott. You must be Carlos DeCosta." He was pointing to the sign on the canopy of the boat that read *Carlos DeCosta's Amazon Charters*.

"Carlos is my father," the young man lied, again with unquestionable confidence. Little did Scott know Carlos DeCosta was floating face-down in a muddy estuary further up the river. "My name is Leandro. Please, after you."

He gestured for Scott to board before untying the boat and pushing them off. The engine fired up once more as Leandro took the wheel and veered away toward the middle of the wide river, to deeper, darker waters.

There were two sliding doors leading into the cockpit, one on either side of the small cabin. They were both open. Scott stood in the port-side doorway, watching the sun leave the treetops and bathe the rainforest in its light and heat.

"So, you want to see *Lago Acarituba*?"

"How do you know?"

"The clerk at the hotel told me when he booked the charter. You must want to see something special down there. Perhaps you're looking for something beautiful, like the pink dolphin. Or perhaps something more dangerous, like the giant green anaconda. The largest snake in the world. He guards the river, you know. The natives consider him a god of the waters."

"So I've heard," Scott said.

Leandro lifted one eyebrow and gazed at him, fishing curiously. "Perhaps a man like you is looking for both. Something beautiful and dangerous at once." Leandro took Scott's silence as consent. "Well then, you've come to the right place."

"If it's all right with you, I think I'll watch the view from the bow," Scott said after a moment, keen to keep his mind focused on his destination and the treasure hidden deep in the jungle.

"Certainly, Mr. Sapphire... I mean, Scott. But don't lean too far over the railing. And tell me if you see any strange ripples on the surface. It'll either be a shift in current... or a school of piranha."

From the stout-nosed bow of the boat, Scott looked across the vast black waters of the Rio Negro, watching the birds flutter out of the trees on the river banks, or fly low across the river, their wings dipping and skimming across the surface. Within the first half a mile, they passed three other riverboats, all circling and buzzing within safe distance of Manaus' ports.

But soon the DeCosta riverboat began to turn right, and the mouth of the Amazon opened wide to starboard.

The black water of the Rio Negro met the wild brown currents of the Amazon in a line so clear, so divided, it was like stepping over a border.

It was the line between civilization—

—and the unknown.

As the boat crossed over from the waters of the Rio Negro and entered the Amazon River, Scott glanced back and saw the flat cityscape of Manaus disappear around the bend. He looked ahead and noticed a quivering motion on the surface of the water, up on the left hand side of the river. He turned to the cockpit cabin and pointed ahead. "Ripples, on the port side."

Leandro stepped out of his cabin and surveyed the river. "Currents," he reported.

Nonetheless, Scott stepped back from the railing and took a seat on an old plank that had been laid across several plastic gasoline drums, acting as a makeshift sitting bench. Carlos DeCosta had not built his riverboat for luxury, but as long as it stayed afloat, Scott didn't care. In fact, he had specifically requested something old and run-of-the-mill, something discreet.

As the sun crept higher and higher, the air grew hot and sticky with the intense humidity. The boat kept to the middle of the wide river, watched by the cautious, suspicious eyes of the tropical toucans and tamarins in the trees, and the still-life alligators basking on the muddy banks.

Scott wiped the sweat from his brow. His shirt was wet with perspiration now. He twisted one or two buttons undone with slippery fingers.

"Take it off," Leandro urged with a laid back shrug.

He had locked off the wheel and left the boat to cruise along by itself, and now joined Scott at the bow. He was himself shirtless—his singlet tucked into the back of his shorts—revealing his solid, brown, glistening torso. "Trust me, you'll be more comfortable."

Leandro took up an empty bucket in one hand, and then opened a hatch in the bow compartment, rummaged about and found a rope. He tied it to the handle of the bucket, then dropped the bucket into the river, let it fill and hauled it aboard. Plucking the singlet from the back of his jeans, he soaked it in the bucket, then used it to sponge down his neck.

His chest.

His hard, gleaming abs.

Leandro noticed Scott's eyes on his tight, tanned torso, Scott's fingers lingering on the last few buttons of his shirt. "Are you shy, Scott? You don't appear to have any reason to be, a man as handsome as yourself."

Scott smiled. "Shy is something I've never been, I'm afraid."

Leandro smiled back. "Good. You won't mind then."

"Mind what?"

But Leandro was already unzipping his shorts, sliding them down his strong thighs to reveal his naked body. His cock, thick and bouncing in a semi-hard state, won Scott's attention instantly.

"Want a drink?" Leandro smirked. "A beer, I mean."

"It's kinda early, don't you think?"

Standing naked before him, Leandro smiled and gestured to the river and the rainforest beyond. "Look where you are, Scott. The middle of jungle. There's nobody here to judge you. And as for time, it doesn't mean a thing out here."

Leandro put down his wet singlet, picked his shorts up off the deck, and pulled a small folded pouch from the pocket. He unrolled it on top of the railing. Scott saw a lighter, paper, tobacco. Leandro rolled a cigarette and slowly licked the edge of the paper, not once taking his eyes off Scott, his tongue lingering, long and wet. He sealed his cigarette with nimble fingers and lit it.

"Do you smoke?" Leandro offered him the cigarette.

"No, thank you."

"Do you mind if I do?"

"Not at all."

Leandro lit his cigarette and said again, "Take off your shirt." He was well on his way to a full erection now, his bountiful cock as handsome as he was. "It'll cool you down. So will a beer. There's an icebox in the cabin. Why don't you bring me one, too, while I pull you in a bucket."

Scott unbuttoned his slinking, sweat-soaked shirt and peeled it off his broad shoulders. He didn't necessarily trust his beautiful riverboat driver, but he also knew he couldn't afford to pass out from heatstroke. Cooling down indeed seemed like a good idea.

As Scott took off his shirt, Leandro eyed him, satisfied with what he saw. He took the cigarette from his lips and blew a plume of fine blue smoke into the air. "That's better." He threw the bucket into the river.

In the cockpit cabin, Scott found the icebox and retrieved a single beer—for Leandro. Scott was already feeling dehydrated, the last thing he wanted was a beer to speed up the process. He began looking for a bottle opener in a drawer of the cabin.

Instead he found a handful of photos. He pulled them from the drawer and flipped through them, assuming the older man in the pictures was Carlos DeCosta: standing proudly at the helm of his makeshift boat; pulling in the anchor; attaching the once brand-new sign that read *Carlos DeCosta's Amazon Charters* to the canopy above a cockpit.

There were other photos too: of a wedding, with Carlos kissing the cheek of a young bride, perhaps his daughter; of Carlos and possibly his wife, holding hands at a dinner table; of Carlos, his wife and daughter, and two other young men, perhaps his sons, in what looked like a family portrait.

Scott suddenly thought it strange that Leandro wasn't in the photo.

In fact, he wasn't in any of them.

Scott opened the next drawer down.

Inside, he found a map of the Amazon, Carlos DeCosta's boat license, and one last photo.

He took in an alarmed breath.

The photo was of Scott himself, a print-out taken from a CCTV security camera in *Mer de l'Hotel D'or* casino.

"Oh, shit."

Scott looked quickly through the window of the cockpit cabin. Leandro was no longer at the bow of the boat.

"What a shame," came Leandro's voice, suddenly close by.

Scott turned sharply.

Leandro was standing in the starboard doorway of the cabin, still naked, cigarette in hand, smiling. His full lips twirled with delight. "I was looking forward to having a little fun before we got down to business, or at the very least a beer. They're icy cold... just like your friend, Dr. Torres. After I finished breaking almost every bone in his body, he fit quite nicely into his refrigerator."

Scott glared at Leandro, his eyes filling with rage. "What have you done? He was an innocent man."

"They're the easiest ones to kill." Leandro laughed. "And I'm guessing *you* want to kill *me* now, don't you? What a pity you didn't get a chance to look through the next drawer down. It has my switchblade in it. The one I'm going to use to cut you open, as soon as you lead me to the orchid."

Scott's eyes glanced at the drawer, almost involuntarily.

"Go ahead," Leandro tempted him. "I dare you."

"I'm a thief, my hands are fast."

"I'm a killer, so are mine."

Like lightning, Scott made a decoy move for the drawer, and then quickly pulled back before grabbing the drawer handle.

Leandro fell for the move. He dropped his cigarette on the deck and lunged for the drawer. But as his fingers clutched the handle, Scott spun the beer bottle in the air, caught it by the neck and smashed the end of it as hard as he could across Leandro's face.

Glass exploded everywhere.

Leandro reeled backward.

The drawer came out in his hand.

The contents of it crashed across the floor.

Scott caught sight of the switchblade, rattling across the cabin.

With the broken beer bottle in one hand, he dropped and reached for the switchblade with the other.

Before he could snatch it by the hilt, Leandro launched at him. He smash-tackled Scott hard. Their torsos locked with a heavy grunt as the two skidded across the glass-littered floor and out the opposite door of the cabin, onto the port side deck of the boat.

Leandro managed to scoop up the switchblade as they tumbled past it.

Scott lost his grip on the bottle.

It clunked and clattered across the deck, and then bounced over the edge of the boat and landed in the water with a loud *ker-plunk*!

The two men rolled into the railing, Leandro on top of Scott, grinning down at him, his handsome, sinister face now dripping with blood and sweat and frothy beer.

He flicked the switch on his knife, and the long seven-inch blade sprang out, glinting in the sun.

"Kill me, and you'll never find the orchid," Scott warned, struggling against his attacker. "You need me."

"I need you alive," smirked Leandro. "That doesn't necessarily mean I need you in one piece."

Leandro seized Scott's wrist, held it high, and then raised his blade, ready to slice off Scott's fingers. "A thief with no fingers. Now that's something I find strangely amusing."

"Laugh at this!"

Scott bunched those fingers into a tight fist and planted it smack in the middle of Leandro's already lacerated face.

Blood spurted from Leandro's nose.

He jerked backward, and Scott threw him off before scrambling frantically along the deck, headed for the bow and away from Leandro.

Dazed and spitting blood, Leandro went after him.

Scott reached the makeshift bench and pulled himself up, but Leandro had him by the leg now and jerked him back down onto the deck.

The switchblade cut the air and sliced across Scott's bare stomach, drawing a thin line of blood straight across his abs.

Scott grunted and clutched the wound before collapsing onto his back and snapping a hard kick straight into Leandro's chest.

Leandro crashed backward again, picked himself up, and lunged once more. This time, he made a stab at Scott's head with his switchblade.

Scott pulled his face out of the way just in time. The knife missed his cheek by an inch and slammed straight into one of the plastic gasoline drums next to Scott's head.

The drum punctured.

Leandro yanked the knife loose, cutting a three-inch gash in the plastic.

Gasoline splashed across the floor and gushed down the deck toward the stern of the boat.

Scott rolled out of Leandro's way and froze when he caught sight of the cigarette Leandro had dropped, still smoldering on the deck beside the cabin door—

—as the river of gasoline streamed directly toward it.

"Oh, God."

Scott sprang to his feet.

He had to get to the cigarette before the gasoline did.

But Leandro had him by the leg again.

He tripped him up and Scott fell forward, slamming face-down into the deck.

He groaned, giddy and hurting, but managed to kick Leandro once and then twice in the stomach, trying to throw him off.

That's when both of them heard it—

Foooomp!

The stream of gasoline hit the glowing embers of the cigarette and ignited.

The fire trail engulfed the deck in seconds, racing up toward the bow.

Leandro leaped backward.

Scott rolled out of the way without a second to spare, clearing a path for the unstoppable blaze as it pounced up the deck and leaped in through the gaping, gushing hole in the side of the punctured gasoline drum.

Scott gasped.

And suddenly, all around him, the air disappeared.

Instantly, every molecule of oxygen was sucked into the fireball that exploded outward, blowing the bow of the boat to smithereens.

Leandro was torpedoed through the air on the port side on the boat, while Scott was catapulted clear over the starboard side, shooting twenty feet into the air before plummeting into the river.

The velocity plunged him deep into the swirling waters of the Amazon.

He couldn't hear a thing. Not the rush of the bubbles, nor the churning of the water, nor the belting beat of his heart. The explosion had deafened him. All he felt was the forceful undercurrents of the Amazon pulling at him, twisting his body, dragging him along, towing him down.

Desperately, he tried to kick his way to the surface.

He pushed and swam as hard as he could, his lungs bursting.

Then, with an almighty splash and a huge gasp of air, he broke the surface.

Frantically, he blinked the water out of his eyes.

He was in the middle of the vast river and being carried along at a swift pace. He looked back and saw the floating inferno of the boat sending up a huge column of billowing smoke into the air, still coughing up small explosions and fireballs as it groaned and sank in charred chunks. Beyond that, on the far riverbank, Scott caught sight of Leandro, splashing and staggering his way out of the river and onto the shore.

Leandro turned—breathless and bleeding, but very much alive—and watched the sinking, smoke-spluttering boat. He caught sight of Scott, his head bobbing in the water, being swept toward an uncertain fate down the world's most dangerous river.

Before Leandro disappeared from view behind the veil of black smoke now filling the air, Scott saw that sinister grin spread across his handsome, bloody face once more.

And then he was gone.

Scott looked back at the burning boat.

He was moving faster than the wreckage was, the blazing

hulk now falling further and further behind him. He hoped that perhaps something—a splintered piece of wood, a burnt life jacket—might float past him. He tread the waters of the fast-moving current as best he could, working hard to keep his head as high above the waterline as possible without exhausting himself, trying desperately to spot any floating debris.

But there were no splintered chunks of wood.

No burnt life jackets.

What he did see, however, made his already pumping adrenalin shift into overdrive.

Thirty feet ahead of him, and moving toward him fast, was a strange ripple on the surface.

Only it wasn't a ripple.

The water was chopping and chattering. Splashing about. Slapping and jittering and dancing. *That's what this was*, Scott thought to himself, *the Amazon's own unique dance of death.*

If Scott Sapphire had to guess what a school of hungry piranha looked like, he guessed he was staring at it right now.

"No, no, no!" he prayed.

But pray as he might, Scott was indeed right.

A swarm of flesh-eating piranha was headed straight for him, driven into a panicked frenzy by the explosion and the scent of Scott's blood in the water from the gash across his stomach. Now those predators of the water were ready to attack and devour anything in their path.

Quickly, Scott looked to the river shores on either side. He was equal distance from both. He could swim right, he could swim left, but if he didn't swim right now—and fast—there would be no escaping the killer fish.

Frantically he put on a burst of speed, arms propelling him through the water, legs kicking as hard and fast as they could, swimming with the current and veering right at the same time. He had the riverbank in his sights, but it was a long way away.

Too far, he thought.

With every second stroke he glanced at the splashing school of hungry beasts.

The tiny carnivorous wave was only twenty feet away. Now ten.

The killer fish were closing the gap faster than Scott could swim. After all, this was their turf, not his. This was their hunting ground—

—and they could smell him now.

Smell his fear.

Taste the blood.

They zeroed in.

The fastest of the school latched onto Scott's sodden boots and drenched cargoes first and began shredding the material. By the time they chewed their way through to the skin, the rest of killer swarm reached his torso and arms.

With razor-sharp teeth, they began gnashing and ripping at his flesh.

Scott tried to keep swimming, but his strokes quickly turned to thrashing as he desperately attempted to fight the killer fish off. But there were too many of them. A hundred, two hundred, three hundred. They swam at him with their ferocious fangs and latched on in clusters, tearing at his chest, his back, his arms, his legs.

The river gushed red.

Scott tried to breathe but took in huge gulps of water.

He tried to swim, but he was sinking fast.

Sinking in a river of his own blood.

The piranha came for his throat, his face.

His hands flailed above the surface a second longer, then were gone, clutching at nothing but endless water.

Several piranha snatched at his groping fingers.

Scott felt their teeth sink in deep.

He felt the stabbing pain everywhere.

He felt the warmth of his own blood.

And then he felt something else.

Someone else's hand grabbing his hand, tighter than anyone had ever seized him.

Pulling him upward now with as much strength as any man could manage, except it wasn't just any man.

Scott's vision was a blur, but as he broke the surface, he saw a small boat and someone leaning far over the edge of it, pulling him out of the piranha-infested water.

He was hauled into the dry, safe boat, his eyes awash with blood.

Scott still couldn't hear anything, and now he could barely see, but before he passed out, he made out a face leaning over him, a face he was only too glad to see.

"Tom? Tom Truman?"

Chapter VIII

Covent Garden, London

In between the stall of an elderly Asian couple frying up noodles and a cantankerous old Scottish woman selling knitted scarves and mitts, a seven-year-old boy with wild black hair and piercing blue eyes stood behind a wooden crate, boldly shouting in his cockney accent, "Roll up! Roll up! Keep your eye on the ball and the money in your pocket!"

Suddenly, the Scottish woman shouted, "Oh, shut yer trap, boy!" She was glaring down at him over a small red kiddie cart with a white pull handle stacked with boxes of knitwear. It was the grumpy old woman's way of carting her goods back and forth. "Why don't you move on? I don't like ya! You ain't nothin' but a little thief. Nobody wants to play yer stupid game."

"I do," said a man walking past the stalls.

He stepped over to the boy's makeshift table as the kid bellowed theatrically, "Step right up and sit right down, sir." The kid turned a bucket upside-down for the man to sit on before setting himself up behind the crate, placing three upturned plastic cups in a row in front of his customer. "Behold, three plastic cups, sir! Nothing underneath."

The boy lifted each cup to reveal, as he said, nothing underneath.

He then pulled a small marble out of his pocket.

"Please watch as I place a marble under the cup in the middle before I start moving the cups around, like so."

The boy moved the cups around, weaving the cups around each other. After a few seconds he stopped.

"For ten quid, I wager you, sir, please choose the cup with the marble underneath."

The man smiled and reached into his pocket to produce his money. "It seems a little too easy," he admitted, putting his cash on the table. "I kept my eyes on it the entire time. It's this one."

The man lifted up the cup on the left.

His confident smile dropped.

There was nothing underneath.

"Oh," he said, disappointed. "I must have blinked. Where was it?"

The boy picked up the cup on the right and the marble rolled out from underneath.

"Well done, lad," the man said, a little resigned. "You won fair and square."

With that, he stood from the bucket and continued on his way.

The boy was eagerly pocketing his winnings when a meek little voice asked, "May I play?"

The boy looked up to see a girl a year or so younger than himself.

Her clothes were frayed, like his.

Her face was smeared with dirt, like his.

And her eyes were blue, just like his.

But unlike him, her legs were twisted. She had two sticks under her arms to keep her upright. He could see she was about to fall from those sticks, so he rushed to help her to the upside-down bucket.

"Of course you can play," he said as he helped her onto the seat. "Do you have ten quid?"

"No," the girl said. "But I can play for more than money."

"What do you mean?"

"Well, if *you* win, I'll give you a kiss. And if *I* win, you'll let me play the game with the next customer who comes along and we split the winnings, fifty-fifty."

The boy's brow scrunched in disgust. "I don't like girls' germs. That doesn't sound like a very good bet to me."

The young girl smiled. "You might learn something."

The boy's mouth twisted uncertainly as he mulled this over, his brow still furrowed. Eventually he agreed, a little reluctant but curious nonetheless, and sat behind the crate. "Right-o, then. Behold, three plastic cups. Nothing underneath. Please watch as I place a marble under the cup in the middle. I move the cups around, like so. Now I wager you, ma'am, for a kiss—"

The boy screwed up his face again.

"—please choose the cup with the marble underneath."

The young girl tapped the top of the cup on the middle. "That one."

The boy lifted it.

There was nothing underneath.

The girl sighed, a defeated little breath escaping her crippled body. "You won," she said.

"Oh, it's okay, you don't have to give me a kiss, really."

"No, a bet is a bet. You won fair and square."

"Why don't we just agree to a handshake?" the young boy negotiated, a little panicked by the thought of a kiss from a girl.

The girl nodded. "Let's."

They two children held out their hands.

The girl shook the boy's hand with more vigor than even he

anticipated.

Suddenly, the marble came rolling down his sleeve, bounced on the crate and fell to the ground.

The boy gasped.

The girl grinned as she lifted the cup on the left, then the cup on the right—

—to reveal there was nothing underneath any of the three cups. With a smile she said, "I think we both just learned a trick or two."

"You knew all along," the boy said. "You knew it was up my sleeve, didn't you?"

The girl continued to grin. "I think this means I won the bet."

The boy whispered in something of a guilty panic, "You want to play the next game? You want to split it fifty-fifty? Fine, just please don't tell anyone about the marble."

"All right then, but I don't just want the next game," the girl negotiated slyly. "I want to be your partner. You take the east side of the markets, I'll take the west. We could double our money."

"How do I know you're any good at this?"

"Just watch me."

A few moments later, the boy hid behind the crates at the back of the noodle stall and watched as the girl brought in the next customer. "Step right up and sit right down, sir," she said as she awkwardly made her way around the crate on her stick crutches.

"Would you like some help?" the gentleman asked her, concerned.

"No, thank you, sir," she beamed theatrically, like a tiny vaudeville actress addressing her audience. "I may not have a home, I may not have legs that work properly, but I have spirit and determination, and I'm determined to entertain you with my game of skill. Are you ready?"

The man nodded and took a seat on the upturned bucket.

"Behold, three plastic cups, sir! Nothing underneath."

The girl lifted each cup before pulling a marble out of her disheveled cardigan pocket.

"Please watch as I place a marble under the cup in the middle. I move the cups around, like so. For ten quid, I wager you, sir, please choose the cup with the marble underneath."

The man picked up the cup on the right.

The marble rolled out from underneath it.

He looked at the girl, his eyes suddenly regretful, almost horrified. "I'm so sorry," he said. "I kept my eye on the cup. I thought it might have been a trick. I was happy to play along with a trick."

But the young girl shook her head, a tear brimming in her eye. "No, sir. There's no trick. You're a clever and handsome young man. It was a game of skill, and you won fair and square."

The girl reached into her cardigan jacket again, as though rummaging for money.

The man shook his hand in the air to stop her. "No, no, please don't." He reached into his own pocket and pulled out two five pound notes. "I'm happy to pretend you won. You really *did* win something, you know."

As he placed the money on the crate and stood to leave, the little girl asked, "Really? What was that?"

The man turned and said, "You won my heart." With that, he left, letting out a deep sigh and smiling, happy that he had done the right thing by the poor little homeless girl.

The moment he was gone, the young boy appeared from behind the noodle crates, his blue eyes wide and his mouth agape. "That was brilliant!" he gasped.

The young girl grinned proudly and handed him five quid. "My name's Sophie," she said.

The boy took the money and shook her hand.

This time no marble fell from his sleeve.

"I'm Scott. And I think this is going to be the start of a beautiful friendship."

Chapter IX

The Amazon River, Brazil

His lips hurt when he opened them to breathe. He opened his eyes and everything was a blur. He squinted, blinked, and tried to focus. And then he saw—

"Tom?"

"Don't move," the C.I.A. agent ordered. "You're hurt."

Scott tried to sit up and saw Tom with a needle and thread, stitching up one of the many gashes on Scott's bare torso. "Ow! Holy shit! What are you doing!"

"I told you not to move! Now lay back down or else..."

"Or else what?"

"Or else I'll shoot you. Is that a good enough reason?"

"You've got a gun? Did you happen to shoot the bastard who did this? Did you see him on the riverbank?"

"All I saw was a pillar of smoke rising from the middle of the river. Then, a burning wreck. Then, blood in the water. And then there was you."

Scott managed to laugh. "You make it sound so romantic."

Tom splashed half a bottle of antiseptic on Scott's wounds.

Scott's entire body spasmed and jolted as he cried out, "Oh, fuck, that hurts!"

"Not as much as an infection from one of these wounds will," Tom advised casually, studying each bite as he stitched. "*Pygocentrus nattereri*. The red-bellied piranha. One of the most ferocious freshwater fish in the world. Savage as all hell, but an important part of the ecosystem. It's all about balance. Out here, if you take something away, you tip the scales toward disaster."

"Speaking of 'out here,' what the hell are *you* doing in the Amazon?"

"I came for the map you stole."

"What map?" Scott asked innocently.

Tom rolled his eyes and pulled the stitches tight.

Scott winced. "Oh, *that* map. I don't have it anymore," he pretended.

"I know. I reached into your pants and took it."

Scott suddenly grabbed at his crotch, feeling for the map that was no longer there.

"If it's any consolation, you gave me a hard-on," Tom grinned, quoting Scott from their last encounter.

With a bite, Tom severed the thread and tied the last stitch off before pulling a glass vial out of his medikit, snapping off the seal and filling a syringe with the fluid inside.

"What's that?" Scott asked.

"Morphine."

"Enough to take the pain away?"

"Enough to shut you the hell up while I get on with my mission. In the meantime, Scott Sapphire, consider yourself under arrest and in my custody."

Instantly, Scott tried to pull away.

But Tom had already slid the needle into his arm.

His vision was a bright blur when he finally managed to open his eyes again. All he could see was white. Gradually, he made out tiny smeared shapes passing across his eyes. He tried to focus and made out wings.

Birds.

He was looking up at the sky.

Slowly, a face blocked out the sun and filled his field of vision.

"Scott? Can you hear me?"

"Tom?" he asked as the handsome features of the C.I.A. agent's face became clearer.

"How do you feel?"

"Where am I?"

"The same place you were last time. On the boat I hired to try and find you."

Scott looked around him. The boat was an old sixteen-foot runabout with an outboard motor and the unscrubbable odor of fish and boat fuel. Tom had switched off the outboard and locked off the wheel, and was now letting the boat drift with the current.

"How do you feel?" Tom asked again.

"Like someone tried to use me as a voodoo doll," Scott said with a groan, looking down at the stitches and gauze bandages dotted all over his torso. "Jesus, there's holes everywhere."

"Fortunately, they're mostly superficial. I got you out of the water before any of them had time to do any major damage. You'll heal fine, you just gotta take things easy."

Scott tried to sit up and grunted with pain.

"I said, take it easy," Tom said. It was clear, however, that Scott wasn't about to lie back down, so Tom helped ease him up into a sitting position.

"I didn't thank you before," Scott said, his voice pained but sincere. "You saved my life."

"Don't thank me 'til we find that temple and get the hell outta this jungle."

"I still don't get it. Why does the C.I.A. want to find the

temple?"

"To stop Oscar Hudson from finding it. I've been tracking the man for longer than I care to admit, intercepting communications, tapping calls. Hudson intends to harness the properties of the Qixoto orchid and manufacture a drug so powerful it'll cure the common cold, yet so addictive it'll have the entire world hooked on it."

"And become the richest man on the planet in the process," Scott said. "So why beat him to the temple? Why not let him find it and catch him in the act?"

"My first job is to find out if the temple, and the orchid, actually exist. The evidence so far is pretty threadbare. A journal. A map. A few stories salvaged from a single voyage down the Amazon by a man deemed insane by the scientific world. Hell, if the temple and the orchid *don't* exist, if Rosso's story is just a myth, then this case is as good as closed and Oscar Hudson and his daughter will hire the best lawyers in the world to get them off the hook for opening fire on a C.I.A. agent in Monte Carlo."

"And if the temple and the orchid *do* exist?"

"Then, I'll destroy the map before Hudson can get his hands on it so that nobody will ever find that place again."

"Someone will find it someday, you know that, right? Nothing stays a secret forever."

"I don't need forever," Tom said. "I just need to stop Oscar Hudson."

Suddenly, Scott stood with a wince. Something had caught his eye. He was looking beyond Tom, pointing to the left back of the river. "Look. Three tributaries in a row." He glanced at Tom. "The third tributary takes us to *Lago Acarituba*."

Scott and Tom both moved to the bow of the boat. Tom turned the key in the ignition, and the outboard revved to life before he turned the wheel to port and headed for the third tributary.

Slowly, the boat entered the side-stream, gliding along the

water as the branches from the trees that grew on both banks of the tributary formed a light-dappled canopy above them. Moss draped down from the branches, along with the occasional bright green boa, watching as the boat passed beneath.

It was cooler beneath the canopy. The sunlight shone in shafts onto the water, filtering through the trees in insect-filled shards of light.

"The map," Tom said to Scott. "It's in the glove compartment."

As Tom continued to steer the small boat left and right through the meandering tributary, Scott pulled the map out, still safe in its watertight plastic sleeve. "So who are you, anyway, Special Agent Tom Truman? How the hell did you wind up in the middle of the Amazon with me?"

Tom glanced at Scott. He smiled at Scott's forthright question. "I can't figure you out. There's something strangely open and honest about you... for a thief."

Scott grinned his charming grin. "I'll take that as a compliment. So does an honest guy like me get an honest answer?"

Tom paused a moment, watching the moss-veiled trees drifting by as he said, "I grew up in Texas, just me and my dad. He was a Ranger. One day, he pulled a guy over for speeding. The guy was speeding because he had a trunk full of cannabis and was headed for the border. He shot my dad twice in the chest. That day, I vowed to one day uphold the law. To learn as much as I could to become someone my father would be proud of. To live up to my namesake, just like my dad."

Scott looked at Tom. With admiration. With pride. And perhaps with a little envy, having never known his own family.

Tom turned to Scott. "You know, it's tough for a kid to grow up alone."

"I know," Scott whispered. "I guess I was lucky. I had it tough, too. But I was never alone."

"So, you heard my story. What about you? What turns an

honest, good-looking guy like Scott Sapphire into a thief?"

Scott couldn't help but smirk.

"I blame chocolate."

Chapter X

Covent Garden, London

Scott and Sophie peered cautiously over the top of a crate full of cabbage, their big blue eyes even bigger as they gazed down the row of stalls, staring at the fancy Belgian chocolatier who had set up a new stand at the north end of the markets.

His name was Monsieur DeRidder. Scott and Sophie had dubbed him 'DeRidder of Children,' for every time a child approached his stall, full of excitement at the sight of his chocolatey delights, the plump and pompous Monsieur DeRidder would hiss and frighten them away. He insisted that his chocolates were so divine, so perfect, that they were intended purely for the refined palates of adults who could not only appreciate them, but more importantly, *afford* them. Yes, even though Scott and Sophie had made enough money from their marble swindling to buy some bread and cheese and even some ham, they still didn't have enough money to taste one of Monsieur DeRidder's delectable treats—not that he would have let them come near his stall in the first place.

God forbid two dirty, homeless children such as Scott and

Sophie should even dare to venture up to his chocolate stall.

Unfortunately, for 'DeRidder of Children,' young Scott loved a good dare.

"I've heard he mixes the tears of angels with swirls of chocolate," Sophie whispered, "then spins them with the golden hair of fairies."

"He kills fairies?" Scott asked, a little devastated.

"I don't know," Sophie answered defensively. "It's just a story."

"Shhh," Scott said, annoyed. "Now here's the plan..."

A few minutes later, Sophie limped her way up to the chocolatier's stall, propping herself up on her stick crutches as she stared into the glass displays containing hundreds of chocolates of all description:

White chocolate.

Milk chocolate.

Caramel chocolate.

Coffee chocolate.

Dark chocolate.

Chocolates full of nuts and berries.

Chocolates covered in silver sprinkles.

Chocolates dusted with chili powder.

Chocolates molded into hearts and diamonds.

Seashells and starfish.

Suns and moons.

Mermaids and marigolds.

Timidly, Sophie held up a few coins.

"Please sir, may I have a—"

Before she could finish, Monsieur DeRidder roared from over the top of his displays, "Be gone, filthy beast!"

Little Sophie whimpered, her eyes wide and terrified. "But please, sir, I have money."

"Not enough! Your money will never be enough! Now get out of my sight, you wretched urchin, before those dirty hands of yours start pawing in vain at the glass."

With that, the rotund chocolatier rushed around to the front of his stall to defend it.

Sophie shrieked and tried to back away fast as Monsieur DeRidder flicked his apron at her as though she were a fly. "Shoo, I say! Get away! Shoo!"

But Sophie and her crippled legs couldn't retreat fast enough.

Suddenly, her stick crutches gave way, and the little girl fell backward.

People all around gasped as they watched the girl tumble to the ground under the abusive words and apron-flick of the Belgian chocolatier.

With a gasp, 'DeRidder of Children' realized he may have gone too far—at least in the eyes of his purchasing public.

Quickly, he swooped down to help the girl.

"Oh, you poor little child," he announced theatrically. "Let me help you up, my little angel. Are you all right?"

Sophie allowed the fat Belgian to assist her up, her eyes glancing back at the chocolatier's stall as she teetered on her weak legs. "Yes, thank you. I'm all right, kind sir," she said.

"Perhaps I could give you a chocolate, just one, to help you on your way," Monsieur DeRidder smiled, more as a declaration of good will to the crowd than the child.

"No!" Sophie shouted, a little too enthusiastically, her eyes still on the chocolate stall. "I'll be happy if you just watch me safely walk away. Thank you, sir."

Without another word, Sophie turned and hobbled away on her crutches.

Under the pressured gaze of the spectating crowd, Monsieur DeRidder watched the girl take each and every slow step back into the marketplace, the fake smile cemented on his face, until eventually, she disappeared.

The moment the little crippled girl had vanished from sight, the crowd turned away and went about their business, at which point Monsieur DeRidder let out an annoyed sigh and turned back to his stall.

As soon as he did, the pot-bellied Belgian let out a scream.

For every single one of his chocolate displays was now completely empty.

That afternoon, Scott and Sophie sat behind the cabbage crates eating some of the finest chocolate in Europe. But instead of shoveling it into their mouths like greedy children, the two homeless orphans ate the chocolates as though each treat was the most precious treasure on earth.

"If we had parents, do you think they would love us?" Sophie asked, her mind wandering on a sweet cloud of chocolates.

"Well, obviously we had parents," Scott said. "Otherwise, we wouldn't be here. We didn't fall from the sky, you know."

"Maybe we did," Sophie whispered hopefully. "Maybe that's what happened to my legs. I must have come in for a crash landing."

She laughed, and Scott laughed with her, his teeth covered in chocolate.

"But seriously," Sophie continued, "if we had parents now, if we lived in a big house, if we were good children, do you think they would love us?"

Scott thought about the question. "Probably not. We do steal from people, after all."

"But only because we don't have parents. And because we don't live in a big house. If we had rich parents who loved us, we wouldn't have to steal. Stealing is for the needy, right?"

"I wouldn't really call us needy," Scott pointed out. "I mean, we're certainly not rolling in opportunities, but I wouldn't call us needy. There's kids starving in Africa who are needy. There's people dying in wars who are needy. There's animals in cages who are needy. You and me, we just have to make our own way, that's all."

Scott could see he'd given poor young Sophie a little too much to think about. He decided to put a chocolate-smeared smile on her face by asking, "But if we did have rich parents, what would their names be?"

Sophie pondered happily over the question. "Prince Theodore and Lady Georgina," she decided with a grin.

Scott nodded approvingly. "They sound rich, all right."

"And they'd buy us chocolates like these."

Scott smiled even more. "I could eat chocolates like these forever."

Sophie giggled. "Me, too!"

Together, the children nibbled delicately on the expensive chocolates, savoring every bite, experiencing every filling—the cherries, the nougat, the hazelnuts, the caramel—with so much joy and appreciation that Monsieur DeRidder would have been proud.

Unfortunately, on the north side of the markets, Monsieur DeRidder didn't give a damn about anything apart from finding the culprit that had stolen his chocolates.

After Scott and Sophie had eaten their fill of chocolates, they stashed the rest of their treasure in a hesian sack under a cabbage crate and returned to their marble and cup trick, Scott heading for the east side of the markets while Sophie made her way to the west.

"Roll up! Roll up!" Scott called from between the noodle stall and the cranky Scottish woman and her scarf stand.

But before another word could leave his lips, he heard a scream.

It came from the west side of the markets.

It was ear-piercing, and whoever was screaming was clearly terrified.

Scott jumped up from behind his crate, sending his plastic cups and marble bouncing over the ground.

From the stall beside him, the Scottish woman appeared. For once she wasn't grumpy. No, this time she was grinning with glee. "Sounds like yer cripple friend's in trouble. Looks like yer game's up, ya little scoundrel."

Panic filled Scott first.

Then rage.

With Sophie's scream still filling the air, he glared at the Scottish woman, and with all his anger, he charged at her.

In a fluster, she stumbled backward before Scott crashed into the boxes stacked on top of her red kiddie cart. The boxes fell on top of the screeching Scottish woman as she hit the ground, an avalanche of knitted scarves and mitts and beanies toppling on top of her.

And suddenly, the kiddie cart was gone.

Scott had the handle in his fist and was racing as fast as he could through the markets, weaving in and out through the cluttered aisles, darting toward the scream that still echoed through the air.

As he turned around a corner of stalls he saw a police officer hauling Sophie off the ground by one arm, as though she were the catch of the day. Beside the officer was the angry chocolatier, shouting, "She's the one! She manipulated me! I can see chocolate on the corner of her mouth!"

Without a second's hesitation, Scott turned the little red wagon in front of him and charged, using the kiddie cart as a battering ram, plowing it straight into the ankles of the police officer—

—who dropped Sophie before tumbling directly into the angry Belgian chocolatier.

With a *thunk,* Sophie landed inside the little red wagon.

With a shriek, the police officer and 'DeRidder of Children' fell to the ground and landed on their backs, their arms and legs flailing like turtles as Scott turned to Sophie.

"You okay?"

Sophie nodded and yelled, "Go!"

The cart rattled and clanged as Scott tore through the markets with Sophie in tow, sending shoppers and stall owners parting left and right as the two children made their frantic, ramshackle getaway.

Behind them they heard a chorus of police whistles.

Scott knew they had to get out of the markets—and fast!

He saw the signs to the Covent Garden tube station and bolted for it, Sophie bouncing and holding on tight to the red wagon behind him.

As Scott cleared the markets, he made a beeline for the tube entrance.

He hit the stairs and raced down them, the cart handle still in his hand, Sophie clinging on tightly as the wagon jolted and bounced down the stairs.

Scott glanced behind him once to see not one, but three police officers in hot pursuit.

He glanced ahead and saw the ticket gate.

Like a baseball player heading for a home run he dropped into a slide, shouting to Sophie, "Duck!"

Scott slid under the ticket gate.

Sophie ducked just in time as the cart rolled at rocket speed under the gate.

Scott jumped to his feet, his hand still clutching the cart handle, and kept sprinting.

He ran as fast as he could along the Piccadilly line platform, commuters jumping out of his way, until finally he reached the end of the road.

No more platform.

Nowhere else to go.

Unless—

Scott turned to Sophie. "Do you trust me?"

Sophie nodded without hesitation.

With all his strength, the seven-year-old scooped Sophie up in his arms before leaping off the platform and onto the tracks.

As the shouts of police officers echoed from the platform behind them, Scott raced into the darkness of the tube tunnel, clutching Sophie as tightly as he could.

A small light appeared in the blackness up ahead.

The tracks on either side of them rattled as a wind blew against Scott's face. The wind quickly turned into a rush of air.

Scott stopped, panting with fear and exhaustion.

Behind them the shouts of police offices and commuters became more frantic.

"Get off the tracks! There's a train coming! Somebody do something—"

But within seconds, the roar of the oncoming train drowned out the shouting voices.

The light of train grew brighter and brighter, shining in Scott's bright blue eyes, turning them into frozen sapphires.

Glittering in what he was certain was his final moment.

He was blinded by the fast-approaching light now, deafened by the rumble of the train and the clanging on the tracks.

Sophie buried her head in his shoulder

Scott gripped her tight and clamped his eyes shut tight.

He didn't see the old maintenance door in the wall of the tunnel quickly slide open, nor did he see the hand reach out and grab him by the shirt.

All he felt was his body being yanked off its feet—his arms still clinging to Sophie as tight as they could—as the train thundered past in an explosion of wind and noise.

At first he thought it was the train that had picked him up off his feet.

But if it had, he'd be dead.

And he wasn't.

Scott felt Sophie still wrapped in his arms.

He opened his eyes and saw the maintenance door slide shut, blocking out the lights of the train as it rushed by.

Quickly, he realized they were no longer on the tracks, but *inside* the wall of the tube tunnel.

And they weren't alone.

"That was awfully close," said a man matter-of-factly, his face illuminated as he struck a match. "You two look like you might be in a spot of bother. Right-o then, let's get you outta here before them police come lookin' for ya. I got a nice little place down near Embankment station. Follow me."

The man started to plod away down the inside of the tunnel, like a mole pottering about his business.

Scott just stood there a moment longer, Sophie still in his aching arms, both of their hearts hammering and their eyes wide in complete shock.

The man noticed that the two children hadn't moved and turned around. "Well, come along, then."

Suddenly, he realized what might be the matter with the two children. "Oh, I'm sorry. I didn't introduce myself. My name's Arthur Dodge, but you can call me Artie. Pleasure to make your acquaintance. Now come along, no time to dilly-dally. Those coppers don't exactly have much of a sense of humor. Trust me!"

Chapter XI

Lago Acarituba, Brazil

The tributary opened out onto the enormous expanse of *Lago Acarituba* just as the sun was setting, turning the entire lake into a caldera of fiery orange. An abundance of birdlife squawked and skimmed the surface of the lake in search of a sunset meal. Fish leaped from the water and splashed back down, sending dusk's red ripples shimmering across the surface. Insects scattered in swarms before being swooped upon by swallows.

Tom switched on a spotlight at the bow of the boat as Scott glanced one last time at the sinking sun before referring to the map.

"I think we have a pretty good idea which way is west. If we follow the eastern rim of the lake it'll lead us to a large channel that winds south. That'll take us into the *igapo* and eventually lead us to Diabo Falls."

Tom steered the boat at a gentle cruising speed while Scott pointed the spotlight to illuminate their path. They veered clear of submerged trees, their branches jutting up out of the black water like the claws of some swamp beast ready to seize the boat and drag them to a watery grave.

As night set in, the darkness came alive.

The branches above were filled with the screeching of howler monkeys and the hissing of tree snakes. In the water, unseen creatures splashed and thrashed, occasionally bumping against the hull of the small boat. River frogs croaked. Giant horned beetles chirped. Vampire bats squealed.

There was no sleeping.

As they steered the boat south into the night, they ate fruit and bread that Tom had brought along.

In time, the blackness began to give way to the dark blue of dawn.

Their surroundings slowly took shape.

They were now at the far end of the southern channel, the trees closing in on both sides, until soon water and vegetation merged and they were in the swamps, surrounded by reeds and water lilies and floating moss. It was impossible to see the water beneath the plant life. There was no telling how deep it was—

—or what was underneath.

"We need to pull the motor up before something gets tangled in the blades," Tom said, cutting the engine. He hoisted up the outboard, and the boat drifted along for a short distance as Tom pulled out the oars. He tossed one to Scott, and then dunked his oar in the water to measure the depth.

He hit the bottom a few feet down.

"We should be able to push ourselves along for a while."

Like gondoliers in a canal in Venice, Scott and Tom began plunging their oars into the water and pushing the boat along.

The sun rose quickly, and the heat bore down on the two men.

Sweat raced down Scott's bare chest and back, soaking into his bandages.

Tom soon pulled off his own shirt which was already drenched and heavy.

Scott looked over at him, smiling as he took in the special agent's broad brown shoulders, his pumped arms and strong chest. "Guess you guys do a lot of working out in the C.I.A., huh?"

"Guess so," Tom said. "And if you keep lookin' at me like that you're gonna do it again."

"Do what again?"

"Give me another hard-on."

"Special Agent Truman, are you coming on to me?"

"No, sir. I'm on a case. That would be... unprofessional of me. Of course, once the case is closed, I may reconsider."

"You mean, sometime *after* we find the temple, but *before* you arrest me."

"Correct. So long as you promise not to knee me in the balls again."

"I think you'll agree I was trying to save your life."

"Are you kidding?" Tom laughed, a look of incredulity on his face. "You almost got us both killed."

Scott's tone became argumentative. "I wasn't the one who took a gun into the situation."

"That gun was the only thing that got us outta there. Otherwise, Ella Hudson would have turned you and me into bear rugs by now! I had the whole thing in hand before you came along."

"And I had *my* hands on both the map and the Golden Egg until you screwed it all up! I could have sold that egg on the black market in seconds. Do you have any idea what I could have done with that money?"

"What? Splashed out on a new condo in the Cayman Islands? That's what wealthy thieves like you do, right?"

"Wrong! I could have made sure every orphan in New York had a turkey dinner and something to give thanks for next Thanksgiving! And trust me, there's nothing wealthy about me."

Tom screwed up his face. "Who the hell do you think you are?

Robin Hood? Well, guess what, you're not! If you think robbing from the rich and giving to the poor makes you a better person, it doesn't. This is just your idea of fun. You can't make everything better. You can't give those orphans what they really need. You can never bring back my dad!"

"What the hell's your father got to do with this?"

"It was lawbreakers like you who took him away from me!"

"Are you saying I'm no better than a murderer?"

"I'm saying you're someone who screws with the system."

"Maybe the system needs to be screwed! And at least you were lucky enough to know who your father was!"

Suddenly, the boat jolted to a halt along with the sharp sound of something scraping against the hull. Scott and Tom both rocked unsteadily before Scott said, his voice still angry, "Great. Now we've hit a snag."

Tom looked overboard. All around them were swamp trees stretching up into the sky, their mossy roots like sea dragons, arching up out of the water before reaching diving deep beneath. "I think we're stuck on the root of a tree," he reported. "We might be able to push ourselves off."

With all their strength, Tom and Scott dug their oars into the bottom of the swamp and tried desperately to free the boat. But after ten minutes, they knew it was no use.

Tom took a deep breath. "I'm going in."

Scott shook his head. "Are you crazy? You don't know what the hell's in that water."

"What do you want us to do, sit in this boat for the rest of our lives?"

Scott shook his head. "I'll go."

"No, you'll infect your wounds."

"Then shoot me full of penicillin when we get the hell outta here."

Scott jumped over the edge of the boat and splashed into the swamp.

That's when Tom heard the sounds of tails swishing through the water from beyond the trees. "Oh, shit."

Beneath the surface, the water was brown and murky and full of dead, drifting leaves and swirling slime. Scott swam under the boat and through the muddy water saw that Tom was right: the boat was wedged on giant, gnarled root. He began pushing against the hull using his arms and shoulder when suddenly, there was another splash in the water.

Amid a frenzy of bubbles and the billow of silt, Tom appeared, eyes wide. He grabbed Scott by the arm and pulled him away from the hull, his legs kicking, his arms pulling him through the water as fast as he could.

Immediately, Scott realized they were in danger.

A second later, he saw them coming.

Alligators.

Dozens of them.

They were speeding through the water from all directions, zeroing in on what promised to be a feeding frenzy.

Tom and Scott both broke the surface and grabbed onto the side of the boat, trying desperately to pull themselves up. But their hands were wet, the boat slippery, and before they could hoist themselves to safety a giant gator slammed into the hull right beside Scott, sending the boat spinning off the root, through the water—

—and out of Scott and Tom's grasp.

The two fell back into the water before Scott gasped, "The trees! Get to the trees!"

Just as Tom began thrashing through the water toward the nearest tree, the jaws of another gator came snapping down toward him. Tom pulled back just as the alligator's teeth clamped shut an inch in front of his face.

At the same time, Scott broke off a low-hanging branch just as a gator lunged for him. As its jaws came down, Scott jammed the broken branch into the reptile's mouth, giving him just enough time to baulk a second gator and scramble onto the twisted roots of the nearest tree.

As Tom's gator swirled about and came in for another attack, Scott reached down, hooked Tom under the arm and hoisted him onto the roots before the gator could take off his leg.

Immediately, the alligators began climbing onto the tangled roots.

Scott and Tom started climbing the tree, pulling themselves from branch to branch, higher and higher, until they were safe from the snapping jaws of the alligators below.

Helplessly, the two watched as their dislodged boat drifted slowly away through the *igapo*. "What the hell do we do now?" Tom asked.

Scott pointed through the trees to a dry embankment at the edge of the swamp a short distance away. "How good are you at climbing?"

"When the alternative is swimming with gators," Tom answered, "I can climb just fine."

From one outstretched branch to another, from one tree to the next, Scott and Tom carefully made their way through the canopy of treetops—at times clambering up trunks to reach the next criss-cross of branches, at times catching each other as the slipped on the mossy wood, sending tree bark falling into the chomping jaws of the gators who followed them the entire way across the swamp—until eventually they reached a cluster of trees far enough over dry land to be out of reach from the alligators.

Swiftly the two men swung down from the branches and thudded onto *terra firma*, their drenched boots squelching as they landed.

"Oh, shit!" Tom gasped. "The map! It's still—"

"—in safe hands," Scott finished for him, pulling the plastic-sleeved map from the pocket of his cargoes. "You didn't think I'd—"

"Shh," Tom interrupted. "Do you hear that?"

Scott's ears were still ringing slightly from the explosion on the charter boat. He shook his head. "Hear what?"

"Listen."

Scott craned his neck, trying to listen for something other than the drone of insects and the caw of birds, until finally, somewhere far off in the distance, he heard it.

The sound of a waterfall.

An hour later, an airboat propelled itself over the *igapo* and slowed to a drift.

Leandro—his face and hands only slightly burned from the blast that had hurled him into the river—leaned out with a boat hook pole and snagged the abandoned runabout.

"Get on board and see if they left the map behind," Ella ordered from the helm. "And try not to blow anything up this time."

As Leandro boarded the empty boat, Ella stepped down from the helm and opened her laptop. She punched away at the keyboard while Leandro stepped back aboard the airboat. "There's nothing."

"That's all right," Ella said, accessing a grid map of the Amazon on her computer. "Last year, Hudson Pharmaceuticals diversified its interests and became a major investor in one of India's privatized satellite research programs."

Ella zoomed in on the grid with a smile.

"If we can't track them by land, we'll track them from the sky."

Chapter XII

Deep in the Amazon Rainforest, Brazil

Scott and Tom followed the sound of the waterfall, over running creeks teeming with frogs, under enormous fallen trees covered in slippery moss, through layers of vines that hung from branches like curtains. Scott pulled the bandages and gauze off his stomach and chest as he walked, the material too sodden now to be of any use; Tom, walking behind him, did the same to the bandages on Scott's back, also plucking off the dozen giant leeches clinging to Scott's skin without so much as a word.

Scott seemed none the wiser, and Tom couldn't help but chuckle.

"What's so funny?" Scott said, stopping on a patch of muddy sand and turning around to look at Tom.

"Nothing," Tom smiled innocently. He quickly dropped the leech in his hand to the ground.

"What was that in your hand?" Scott asked suspiciously.

"Nothing."

They both quickly looked down.

Indeed, it appeared to be absolutely nothing, for the leech

was nowhere to be seen.

Scott relaxed.

But now Tom's voice took on a suspicious tone. "Where'd it go?"

"Where'd what go?"

Tom looked back up at Scott, suddenly conscious of the fact that he was doing exactly that—looking up.

The two men were roughly the same height, but in the last few seconds, Scott was suddenly two inches taller than Tom. Or rather, Tom was suddenly two inches shorter.

Three inches.

Four.

"Oh, fuck," Scott and Tom both said at once. "Quicksand!"

Tom instantly looked down to see that his boots had vanished into the wet sand.

Scott instantly looked up and saw a low-hanging vine.

He reached up and snatched it just as he felt his own feet sink into the earth.

He pulled on it hard, and the entire length of vine came tumbling out of the tree and flopped onto the sand like a dead snake.

At the same time, both Scott and Tom sank up to their knees in the quicksand.

Desperately, Scott tried to pull his legs out.

"Don't do that," Tom warned. "You'll sink even faster. Whatever you do, don't struggle."

"What else am I supposed to do?"

Scott kept fighting against the sand.

Suddenly, a huge bubble of air exploded on the muddy surface, and he dropped into the quicksand up to his waist.

"Now will you listen to me?" Tom growled.

"Okay, okay, stop being such a smart ass and get us out of here!"

"Pass me that vine. Quick."

"I hate to break the news to you but it's not attached to anything."

"It will be soon. I'm from Texas, remember."

As Scott handed Tom the vine, the young C.I.A. agent quickly started tying the end of it into a lasso knot. He spotted an old rotting log on the edge of the pit of quicksand.

With a deep breath he twirled the lasso vine over his head, and hurled it at the log

It snagged the far end of it.

Tom pulled tight and the lasso tightened around the log.

He laughed triumphantly just before sinking into the muddy sand up to his waist. He turned to see the quicksand was already midway up Scott's torso.

"Grab hold of my shoulders," Tom said, and with one mighty heave he hauled on the vine.

Only, instead of pulling the two of them out of the quicksand—

—all he did was dislodge the log and expose the enormous ants' nest beneath it.

As the log rolled away from the nest, a thousand giant ants with razor-sharp pincers poured out from their exposed mound.

"Remind me never to come here on vacation," Tom breathed in horror.

"They're just ants, right?" Scott asked, hoping against hope.

Tom shook his head. "No, they're army ants. They can kill and devour a wild boar in under ten minutes."

"So, they're kinda like piranhas," Scott gulped. "But on land."

Tom nodded. "I would say that's an accurate description."

"Then, I would say we need to get the fuck out of here!"

As the army ants began to pour across the surface of the quicksand, a brave few sank into the mud while the others marched quickly over the sinking bodies of the fallen, forming a moving, scurrying bridge that made its way toward the two humans trapped in the sand and about to become dinner.

"Pull the vine!" Scott shouted, sinking up to his chest now. "Get the vine back!"

Tom yanked at the vine.

The log swiveled on the ground and the vine came loose.

"See if you can hook the branch above us."

"It's too high."

"It's all we've got!" Scott argued.

As the bridge of ants stretched closer and closer—as Scott and Tom sank deeper and deeper—Tom hurled the vine high toward the gnarled old branch hanging over the quicksand, trying to hook one of its knotted limbs.

He missed and sank another inch into the sand.

Tom threw the vine upward again.

Again he missed, sinking up to his nipples.

In another few seconds he wouldn't be able to move his arms enough to throw the vine. He knew he only had one more shot.

With his best aim, Tom threw the vine one last time.

The lasso looped around a knotted stump.

"Got it!" Tom shouted, turning back to see Scott sinking up to his neck, holding his arms as high as he could.

Tom pulled hard on the vine.

But instead of securing the knot—

—the old branch, all twenty feet of it, was ripped from the tree and came crashing down.

Scott and Tom covered their heads as the branch smashed down beside them, splatting some of the ants before the rest of them scurried up onto the fallen limb and continued on their way to their prey before it disappeared.

"Oh, great," Tom uttered.

But Scott was grinning. "Great! This is great!" He was turning his head as best he could from left to right. "Look at the ants!"

"I'm trying not to!"

"They're crossing over the branch. Look at it. Both ends landed on safe ground. Come on!"

Scott grabbed the branch and started pulling himself toward the far end of the quicksand pit and away from the fast-marching ants.

Tom did the same, glancing back to see the ants gaining on them quicker than they could haul themselves out of the sucking sand.

The muscles in their arms burned.

Their bodies were heavy, the mud like concrete, trying to drag them down.

With one hand, then the other, Scott pulled himself along the length of the branch, closer and closer to the edge.

Tom was only a few inches behind him.

The first of the army ants ran over Tom's hand, up his arm and started digging its pincers into his neck. It was followed by one, two, five, a dozen more ants.

Another dozen bypassed Tom and headed straight for Scott, their pincers piercing his fingers, his hands, his forearms.

As trickles of blood began to flow, Scott reached the edge of the quicksand pit. With all his strength, he pulled himself halfway out of the killer sand before reaching back and grabbing Tom. He hauled as hard as he could, dragging Tom out of the suction of mud until they both clambered out of the deadly mire.

But it wasn't over yet.

The ants continued biting and eating and drilling into their flesh.

"The waterfall," Scott gasped.

With Tom in one hand, he pulled them both to their feet and sprinted toward the sound of the falls. They slapped past giant leaves, leaped over logs, leaving a trail of quicksand through the rainforest until they reached the boulder covered banks of a large, deep, crystal clear waterhole with three separate waterfalls plunging into it from an enormous height.

Without stopping, Scott dived into the water, followed a second later by Tom.

Instantly, the killer ants were flushed off their flesh, drowning in the waters as Scott and Tom swam into the middle of the pool, leaving a swirling stain of mud on the water that quickly washed away with the flow of the falls.

"Are you okay?" Scott said, treading water and catching Tom in his arms.

"Yeah," Tom nodded. "You?"

His hands slid behind Scott's head, his fingers squeezing Scott's hair.

At the same time, Scott took Tom's face in his hands.

"I'm okay now."

With that he planted his lips on Tom's.

Tom moaned and plunged his tongue inside Scott's mouth.

Their legs kicked and entwined in the deep of the waterhole.

Their nostrils flared for air.

While behind them, the three cascades of Diabo Falls plunged into the crystal pool.

On the large flat boulders surrounding the waterhole, Scott and Tom pulled each other ashore, their cargoes and boots dripping wet, their lips sealed in a string of deep, passionate kisses.

As the sun spilled down upon the pool, casting rainbows of all shapes and sizes across the three waterfalls, Tom laid himself flat on his back against the warm rock and kicked off his drenched boots.

Hovering over him, Scott heeled off his own boots before groping his way down Tom's tensed torso to find the buckle of his cargoes. He unsnapped his pants as his eager hand slid inside in search of real treasure.

And there it was, trapped inside Tom's briefs—six, seven, eight inches of prime Texan meat.

Tom groaned into the kiss as Scott squeezed the stiff, thick shaft inside Tom's underwear.

With his thumb, Scott kneaded the head of the cock beneath the cotton and a large burst of pre-come soaked through the already wet material. Scott smeared it over the bulbous head, pronouncing the shape and size of the cock's crown.

He pulled his lips away from Tom's but continued kissing, his mouth pressing against the stubble on Tom's chin, his tongue tasting the sweat on Tom's throat. He licked and kissed his way further south, mauling Tom's large chest as it rose and fell in quick gasps, teething and biting and hardening Tom's nipples before sliding down the mounds of his abs.

At the same time, Tom seized the locks of Scott's black hair, trying to steer his handsome face straight down to his aching bulge.

But Scott pulled away from Tom's grasp, settling back on his haunches before standing up in front of Tom, the crotch of his own cargoes now huge and pulsating. He reached into one of his pockets, pulled out a condom packet and tossed it onto Tom's panting abs.

"I'm a good Boy Scout," Scott winked. "I always come prepared for come."

"Something tells me you were never a Boy Scout."

Scott grinned. "Shut up and put it on, Special Agent Truman."

As Scott stood, unbuckling his cargoes, Tom frantically slid both thumbs between his hips and the waistline of his briefs and cargoes and pushed them down his legs, stripping himself naked.

His cock sprang upward from a thatch of trim blond pubic hair and smacked against his stomach.

It was thick and long, with a subtle lean to the left.

Scott smiled approvingly. "I thought you might have been

left-handed when I saw you with your gun, but now I'm certain."

"What do you mean?"

Scott made a jerking-off motion with his left hand. "Your teenage years are showing. It's amazing how a young man can shape his own cock."

Tom grinned and ripped open the condom wrapper. "So long as it fits up your ass, I'm happy."

The crystal blue of the waterhole, the sapphire blue of Scott's eyes, this strange, exotic, beautiful, dangerous setting—all of it made Tom want Scott even more. His cock jerked and bobbed as he rolled the condom down his thick, curved shaft.

Standing before him, Scott unbuckled his cargoes and eased them down over his hips.

He wasn't wearing any underwear.

The cargoes slipped down to reveal his dark manicured pubes. They slid a little further to expose the thick-veined stem of his shaft. Inch by inch, Scott revealed more and more of his cock, stiff as a rod, pointing downward until his cargoes rolled over the plum-sized head of his cock, releasing it with a spray of pre-come as the shaft pounced free.

With that handsome smile fixed to his face, Scott tugged and jerked at his beautiful hard cock as a show for Tom, squeezing the head and forcing another jewel of pre-come from the slit which dropped onto Tom's thigh.

Then, without another second's hesitation, he set one foot beside Tom's right hip, and one foot beside his left, and lowered himself down, the muscles of his thighs bunching up, strapping and strong.

As he descended, Scott wet his hand with his mouth, drenching his fingers with his tongue, before reaching down and moistening the condom covering Tom's thick, long cock.

Seizing the shaft in his wet fist, he stroked a moan out of Tom, who rolled his head back and closed his eyes.

He guided the head of Tom's shaft toward his open, yearning ass.

Tom groaned again as his cock nudged between Scott's cheeks, spread wide to take Tom in.

With a deep breath, Scott eased himself down on Tom's shaft, just an inch or so before he let out a moan of pleasure, relaxed his body completely and melted all the way down Tom's cock.

As he did so, Scott's dick slapped up against his stomach, wanting some attention of its own.

Tom saw and seized it in his fist, touching the engorged shaft for the first time. The veins pulsed under his grip. He began stroking it, forcing a moan out of Scott who watched as Tom's fist slid up and down the stretched skin of his shaft, squeezing hard, moving faster and faster.

As Tom jerked him off, Scott began sliding up and down Tom's thick, long dick. He exhaled mightily with each descent, emptying his chest as Tom's cock filled his ass, before inhaling deeply as he raised himself high and plunged down upon Tom's cock once again.

Again and again.

His pace quickening.

Becoming hungry and reckless.

Slapping himself down onto Tom's hips faster and harder.

In response, Tom picked up his pace on Scott's throbbing cock until Scott demanded through gritted teeth, "Make me come!"

Tom's fist became a blur.

Scott leaned forward, still riding the Texan as hard as he could, his hands clenching the tight-muscled pecs of Tom's chest. He felt the drumbeat of Tom's heart beneath his right palm.

It was enough to make Scott's balls erupt.

In an explosion of white, come fountained through the air from Scott's cock like bubbles from a champagne bottle. The hot fluid splashed all over Tom's stomach and chest.

The second Tom felt the heat of Scott's loins hit his body, his own balls burst, sending a rush of come up his shaft as Tom arched his back and let out a rapturous roar.

High in the trees above, birds took flight and monkeys howled.

Scott and Tom didn't hear a single shriek, their heads filled with the pounding of blood through their temples as they both came again and again.

Scott's seed drenched Tom's gut and chest.

Tom's seed filled the condom until he thought it might burst.

Then, slowly, breathlessly, the two let out a sigh.

Tom sank against the rock.

Scott sank against Tom, smearing his come between their two heaving stomachs.

He still felt the pounding of Tom's heart beneath his right palm.

He heard the pounding of the three waterfalls plunging into the crystal waterhole.

And he whispered, "Wanna take a shower together?"

Water cascaded all around them as Scott and Tom stood naked and waist-deep in the waterhole beneath the middle waterfall. The sound of the waterfall was loud, but the two spoke softly, their faces close.

Tom kissed Scott's lips gently before pulling back and gazing into his eyes. "You're something very... unique, Scott Sapphire."

Scott smiled. "And your eyes are like chocolate."

"You like chocolate, don't you?"

"No," Scott said, shaking his head. "I *love* chocolate. I like to fill my life with guilty pleasures. I think you might be my latest."

The two kissed again until Tom pulled back, abruptly this time. Scott could see there was something on his mind.

"Tom? What's wrong?"

Tom hesitated before answering. "There's something I need to tell you."

He took a deep breath, opened his mouth to speak, but suddenly another voice broke the moment between them, shouting from the edge of the falls.

"How romantic!"

Scott and Tom both turned sharply to see Ella Hudson standing on the rocky bank of the waterhole, a gun held casually in one hand, a small backpack slung over one shoulder and an imperious smirk on her glossy red lips. Beside her stood Leandro, his gun trained straight at Scott.

"I hope we haven't interrupted anything too intimate?" Ella asked in a mocking tone.

"Sorry," Scott answered. "You already missed the party."

"On the contrary. The party's only just beginning." Ella gestured to their clothes on the edge of the waterhole and said to Leandro, "Find the map."

After fishing through pockets, Leandro pulled the plastic-covered map out of Scott's cargoes.

Ella looked from the map back to Scott and Tom. "Sorry, boys, but bath-time is over. We've got a temple to find, and you're coming with us." Her smile widened. "If anything in that temple is booby-trapped, you two will be the first to find out."

Under the curious and watchful gaze of the sloths and squirrel monkeys in the trees, the four humans made their way through the rainforest, a rare sight this deep in the Amazon. They walked a straight line, one behind the other, with Ella in the lead, followed by Scott then Tom, both with their hands clasped behind their heads, while Leandro brought up the rear, his gun trained on Tom and Scott the entire way.

Eventually, Scott broke the silence, his eyes on Ella's ass. "You know, I have to admit, you've got a great ass. If I were remotely interested in women I could totally fall for you. I'd probably even follow you willingly into the depths of the Amazon... at gunpoint... battling through the rainforest toward certain death." Scott suddenly reacted to his own words as though he just had a light-bulb moment. "Oh, wait a minute. I forgot. You're a total cunt. That's a deal-breaker, I'm afraid."

Ella shook her head, amused, without so much as turning around. "If you're trying to distract me, Mr. Sapphire, you're wasting your time."

"Then let me give it another try by asking what you intend to do with us if and when we do find the temple."

"To be honest, I'd love to leave you in the jungle and see which of the Amazon's hungry inhabitants finishes you off first, but you seem to be so damn resilient, I'd hate to leave your deaths to chance. Which is why we're all leaving this jungle together.

"I hope you packed a few bandages. It was hard enough getting here alive, let alone getting out again."

Ella shook her head. "Fortunately, we're not going back the same way we came. There's a GPS locator wired into the laptop in my backpack. My father is tracing our every move from his helicopter. Once we have the orchid, we're all taking a trip back to Rio where we can dispose of the two of you properly."

"I hate to point out the obvious," Scott said, "but kidnapping me is one thing. Kidnapping a C.I.A. agent on the other hand... don't you think you're going to draw a little attention to yourself?"

Finally, Ella stopped and turned, a grin of surprise and glee spreading across her face. The other three stopped in her wake as Ella glanced from Scott to Tom and back again. "He hasn't told you, has he." It wasn't a question, more of a realization.

Scott's brow furrowed. He looked at Ella, then turned to Tom. "Told me what?"

Ella laughed. It was a loud, amused laugh that sent the monkeys in the trees shrieking. "I hate to break it to you, but I did a little research after Monte Carlo. There is no Special Agent Tom Truman. It's just plain old Mr. Truman, right Tom?"

She looked at Tom who hung his head in shame. "I'm sorry, Scott. I wanted to tell you back at the waterfall."

"Tell me what?" Scott asked softly, unable to fight off a stabbing sense of betrayal. "Why did you lie to me?"

"Because right now," Ella answered for him, turning back to the trail and pushing her way past the wide fronds of a prehistoric fern, "your little boyfriend here is as much a fugitive as you are. That's why."

"Scott, it's not what you think," Tom said. "I can explain."

Ella froze in her tracks. "Explain later," she said before announcing to the others, "I think we just found the temple."

Scott, Tom, and Leandro hurried up behind Ella, pushing aside the fern fronds to find that Ella who was now standing at the edge of a rocky ravine. Directly in front of them, spanning the ravine, was a primitive, dilapidated suspension bridge constructed from frayed vines and rotting logs from the rainforest, half of them missing. And at the other end of the bridge, almost entirely consumed by the rainforest, were the remains of a large stone temple, its pillars, walls, and steps covered in the most luminous green flowers any of them had even seen.

Ella took a determined step toward the suspension bridge, her face smiling, her eyes fixed on the temple on the other side of the ravine.

Suddenly, Scott took his hands from behind his head and grabbed Ella's arm, jerking her backward.

Leandro shoved his gun into Scott's back. "Don't move."

"I was about to say exactly the same thing to Ella," said Scott. He was looking down at Ella's boots.

Everyone else's eyes followed Scott's gaze.

At first, they saw nothing.

Then, ever so slowly, the creeping, hairy leg of a giant

tarantula felt its way up the toe of Ella's boot. It was followed by another leg. And another. Until the whole damn spider appeared, its black furry body the size of a large rat.

Ella screamed and kicked her leg, sending the spider flying over the ravine.

"Where's the map?" Scott demanded.

Ella nodded to Leandro, who pulled the map out of his pocket and handed it to Scott. They all looked at the sketch of the bridge that Rosso had drawn and realized that his web-like illustration was no metaphor.

Scott handed the map back to Leandro, who returned it to his pocket. "I don't think this bridge is the only thing spanning this ravine," Scott said.

Cautiously, all four of them inched their way to the edge of the ravine and looked down. There was no bottom in sight—

—because twenty or so feet below the bridge and crawling with hundreds of thousands of tarantulas, was a giant tapestry of webs so thick that it stopped the light of day reaching the bottom of the ravine.

It was a net that stretched from one side of the ravine to the other.

A trap.

Filled with the half-devoured carcasses of bats and birds—

—as well as skeletons of several humans that had fallen into the ravine over the centuries. No doubt some of them were Qixoto tribesmen, and perhaps even some of Rosso's men had met their fates here, their deaths long and agonizing as the spiders slowly picked their corpses clean, leaving nothing but bones.

Ella grabbed Scott and pushed him toward the suspension bridge. "You go first," she ordered.

"But I'm a gentleman! It's rude not to let a lady—"

Ella shoved her gun in his face. "You should know by now, I'm no lady. Think of this gun as my dick. And if you don't move,

I'm gonna shove it straight in your mouth and blow my load."

"Okay, okay," Scott conceded. "I'll go first."

Scott swallowed hard and sized up the rickety ancient bridge in front of him. Slowly, he put one hand on the vine railing. He eased one foot onto the first log, and then the other foot. Instantly, the vines holding the bridge pulled and strained to accommodate his weight, like strings on a puppet.

"I suggest we take this one at a time," Scott said with another anxious gulp. "I don't know how much weight this thing will hold."

"I don't think we're going to have time for that," Ella said.

She was looking down at the net of webs which suddenly came alive more than ever. The tarantulas had sensed the movement of the bridge above. And they were mobilizing. Crawling quickly along their webs, spinning new ones, climbing the walls of the ravine, scurrying up toward some fresh meat.

Ella pushed Scott further along the bridge with a forceful nudge of her gun before hastily joining him. "Move!"

With each hurried step, Scott tried to test the strength of the rotting logs before putting his full weight on them.

Ella concentrated hard, following exactly in his footsteps, trying not to look at the moving web below them.

With a shove of his gun, Leandro pushed Tom onto the bridge and followed close behind.

The vines pulled tighter as the weight of all four of them turned the bridged into a precarious, swaying tightrope. The wood beneath their feet creaked. The taut vines groaned.

Halfway along the bridge, a rotten log beneath Scott's left foot broke.

His leg went straight through the hole.

He grabbed the vine railing and caught himself from falling.

The broken log fell into the webs below like a trapeze artist bouncing into a net.

A hundred spiders descended on the piece of wood while Scott watched, knowing next time it might very well be him down there.

"Move faster!" Ella barked behind him.

At that moment, a support vine above them snapped, unable to take the weight.

The entire bridge shifted.

All four of them grabbed for the vine railing as the bridge swung left and pitched right.

That's when one of the tarantulas appeared from under the railing and crawled onto Ella's hand as she held onto the vine for dear life.

Its legs were as long as her fingers.

Ella screamed again.

She let go over the vine, shook the spider off, and lost her footing.

Her scream turned to a terrified gasp as she toppled off the dilapidated bridge.

Scott spun about, dropped to his knees on a creaking log and swooped down with one arm, managing to catch Ella's free hand, her gun still in the other.

Instantly, her fingers started to slip out of his.

"Give me your other hand!" Scott shouted at her. "Let go of the gun! I can't hold you!"

PA-TWANG!

Another vine above them snapped.

The entire bridge swayed and dropped several feet.

Ella screamed, dropped her gun, and reached up with her other hand.

The next in line, Tom was already on his knees grabbing for Ella as well.

The bridge let out another loud groan.

Scott glanced at Tom, their faces close. "This whole bridge is about to collapse."

"I know."

Together they tightened their grip on Ella and with all their strength hoisted her back up onto the bridge as fast as they could.

By now, tarantulas were everywhere, crawling over the vines, scampering over the logs.

Scott jumped to his feet and started leaping across the bridge, dancing from one log to the next, no time to test their strength. He simply hoped for the best.

Ella followed close behind, as did Tom and Leandro.

They jumped and bounded over the tarantula-covered logs as fast as they could.

They grabbed at the vines as spiders scurried for their clutching hands.

As the bridge lurched and listed, more vines snapped, coming down left and right.

Scott saw the edge of the ravine ahead.

He leaped off a breaking log, sprang into the air, and jumped to safety.

Glancing back, he saw the whole bridge starting to come down.

He grabbed Ella and hauled her onto the safe ground, before shouting, "Tom! Run!"

Leandro's hand fell hard on Tom's shoulder and pulled him backward so that Leandro could save himself first.

With a thunderous crack, the center of the bridge broke in two.

Scott heard a sound like firecrackers as every vine supporting the two sections of the bridge snapped apart.

Leandro leaped to safety.

At the same time, Scott dived onto the ground at the edge of the ravine just as the bridge tore apart and collapsed, its ropes and logs slamming against the wall of the ravine on each side.

Clinging to the vines, Tom smashed against the rocky wall.

His fingers and knuckles slammed into the rock.

He lost his grip.

But suddenly Scott had him.

Reaching as far as he could over the edge of the ravine, Scott's hand snatched Tom's wrist tight.

"I gotcha."

Tom looked up, panting, smiling with relief—for a moment.

On all sides, tarantulas were scurrying along the ravine wall, coming at him from left and right.

Digging his boots into the rocks, Tom pushed himself upward as fast as he could while Scott pulled, dragging Tom up onto the brink of the ravine where the two collapsed on their backs.

They watched as the spiders crawled up over the edge after them, but the tarantulas did not dare to stray too far from their webbed ravine. One by one, they turned away and climbed back down to their deadly lair.

"Don't think that just because you saved my life I've changed my mind about killing you both," Ella declared, standing over Scott and Tom. She took Leandro's gun from him and pointed it at them. "Now get up!"

Scott helped Tom to his feet and dusted himself down. "I figured letting you die wasn't exactly gonna get us a seat on your father's helicopter. And given the fact that the bridge is now the domain of ten thousand giant tarantulas, I don't see any other way out of here."

"Correct you are," Ella smiled, waving her gun and gesturing them toward the temple. "Gentlemen, after you."

As Scott turned to the temple, the multitude of brilliant green Qixoto orchids shimmered, turning his sapphire eyes aqua. It was a truly dazzling sight: an ancient temple, its snake sculpted pillars covered in moss and the mesmerizing green orchids sprouting from every inch of stone. Alone, each flower seemed so delicate, yet *en masse,* they had dominated this mighty stone structure. The orchids had reclaimed the temple built in their honor.

Slowly, Scott and Tom made their way toward the overgrown structure, with Ella and Leandro close behind.

Scott stepped first up the three stone steps leading into the temple.

He took a deep breath as he passed the pillars, the angry, orchid-covered faces of two stone snakes hissing at him from either side.

"The green anaconda," Tom whispered from close behind Scott's ear, recognizing the snake in the detailed carvings.

"Apparently, they're the guardians of the temple," Scott said.

"Thank God they're only made of stone."

"Don't speak too soon," Scott warned.

Warily, they stepped over the orchid-dripping threshold of the temple and into a large antechamber. It was a stone-walled room with its roof only partially constructed to let in the bright light of the hot Amazon sun.

Cascading from every wall were countless Qixoto orchids, the daylight shining on their luminous petals and bathing the entire antechamber in rippling green light.

But it wasn't the orchids that Scott was focused on.

It was the large, eight-inch-tall emerald in the center of the chamber—sitting atop of a four-foot-high snake pillar—that had Scott transfixed and put the smile on his face. The emerald had been carved roughly in the shape of an orchid, its petals imperfect and now slippery with moss here and there. And yet it was the most beautiful thing he had ever seen.

Behind Scott and Tom, Ella and Leandro entered the antechamber, their eyes lighting up at the sight of the orchids—as well as the emerald.

Hurriedly, Ella pulled off her backpack and knelt.

She pulled out a pair of tweezers and a glass cylinder with a tiny green light at its base, and opened its lid.

The green light turned red, and frozen mist escaped to the cylinder.

With it, she walked, almost in a trance, to the nearest wall, her eyes set on one of the thousands orchids growing from the cracks in the stone.

Her hand steady, her quest almost complete, Ella reached for the tiny green orchid, clamped it with the tweezers, and gently—but firmly—plucked it from the stone wall, roots and all.

A breath of exhilaration escaped her as she placed it in the cylinder and sealed the lid, the red light instantly switching back to green.

Excitedly she spun about, confident and in control.

"The orchid is ours," she declared triumphantly, marching back to her backpack and placing the cylinder inside. She then stood and turned to the shimmering emerald in the center of the room. "And I think I'll be taking this one as well. For myself."

Scott shook his head. "Ella, wait. There's normally a trick to these things."

Ella laughed off his warning. "Like what? You think the Qixoto installed a security alarm?"

Scott nodded. "Yeah, something like that."

Ella ignored him.

Scott glanced at Tom and whispered, "Get ready to run."

He watched Ella strut straight toward the jeweled sculpture and eye it possessively, before taking it in her hands and lifting it off the snake pillar.

Scott grabbed Tom's hand, ready to bolt.

But as Ella raised the priceless emerald off the pillar—

—nothing happened.

She turned to her backpack, placed the jewel inside and smirked at Scott. "I guess all it needed was a woman's touch."

The floor of the temple began to rumble.

The grin fell from Ella's face.

Behind her, she heard the sound of stone grinding against stone, and turned to see the snake pillar descending into the floor of the chamber.

Scott tightened his grip on Tom's hand and started to run, but not fast enough.

With a loud crack, the edges of the stone floor detached from the walls, letting out a gust of swamp stench that billowed up the walls in clouds.

A split second later, the floor dropped away from the walls altogether.

It tilted downward from the edges, like an umbrella closing, sending Scott, Tom, Ella, and Leandro toppling and tumbling down the slanted stone, spitting them against the rocky wall of a hidden chamber below, before each of them fell, one by one, onto a steep stone spiral slide—carved in the shape of a giant snake.

First Scott, then Tom, then Ella and Leandro sped down the back of the enormous stone snake's back, sliding at an unstoppable pace into a chamber that may never have seen the light of day.

Now, rays of sunlight poured down from the floorless antechamber above.

Scott looked ahead as he hurtled down the slide.

He saw water below him and held his breath.

As he flew off the tail of the stone snake, Scott was hurled through the air and landed twelve feet below in a splash of murky, swamp water.

With a gasp, he broke the surface and staggered to his feet, standing in the chest-high water just as Tom came flying through the air and crashed straight into him, sending them both underwater before they came to the surface, spluttering and coughing.

Scott pulled Tom aside as Ella went sailing by with a scream and a splash, followed by Leandro.

Her dark long hair slicked back and her mascara running, Ella burst from the water with a panicked gasp of air.

Leandro surfaced not far from her.

"Where are we?" Ella shouted.

"Someplace we wouldn't be if you had listened to me before snatching the damn emerald," Scott answered angrily.

He looked around to size up their surroundings.

They were in a pit with swamp water up to their chests, the walls too steep to climb. The tail on the stone snake slide was too high to reach. Far above them, the sunlight shone down from the floorless antechamber, daring them to find another way out for their reckless actions.

As the disturbed water slapped and splashed against the walls of the hidden chamber, Tom turned to Scott. "I'm sorry I lied to you. Only I didn't lie. I *was* C.I.A. when I met you on the boat in Monte Carlo."

"You don't have to tell me now," Scott said. "Let me try to get us out of here first."

"What if we *don't* get out of here?" Tom said. "I want to tell you what happened. So you don't think less of me."

"If we don't get out of here, I'm not going to be thinking about much at all," Scott said.

"Then let me say this now. My father, the Texas Ranger, was killed by one of Oscar Hudson's illegal drug-runners. My whole life I've spent trying to stop Hudson's ventures. Trying to stop him from making money out of the illegal trafficking, the drug experiments, the things that cost innocent people their lives. After the incident in Monte Carlo, the C.I.A. fired me. They disavowed me. They said I'd gone too far. They wanted to take me in for questioning. But I knew I'd never get this close to catching Oscar Hudson again."

Across the watery pit, Ella grinned. "And now look at you. On the run."

"The way I saw it, I had a job to finish!"

Ella simply laughed. "I can't tell you how easy it was to turn the 'good guys' against you. Twenty thousand dollars went into your superior's bank account, and you got tossed out with the trash."

Tom gritted his teeth. "Why you fucking—" He charged before his sentence was done, wading furiously through the water at Ella.

Something else under the surface moved, sending a swirl of currents eddying through the water.

Tom froze.

Everyone looked at the spinning currents of water in the center of the pit.

Leandro looked at the others and whispered, "What the hell was th—"

Something pulled him under the water with such speed and force that the young Brazilian disappeared in a swirl of gurgles and bubbles.

Ella screamed and tried desperately to scramble up the rock wall, still clutching her backpack in one hand.

Scott grabbed Tom and hauled him back against the wall.

"What the fuck?" Tom gasped in wide-eyed horror.

A huge green serpentine back rose through the water like a sea monster.

"It's an anaconda," Scott breathed. "We gotta get out of here."

In an explosion of water, Leandro was jettisoned through the air. He slammed against the rock wall and fell into the water before frantically picking himself up, sucking in a lungful of air.

The body of the green serpent began whirling and spinning through the black water before disappearing once again.

Beneath the tail of the stone snake slide, Scott gave Tom a leg up. "Quick! Try to reach the tail!"

A few feet up the slippery rock wall, Ella lost her grip and splashed into the water. She came up gagging on the foul swamp water before quickly hooking her backpack onto her shoulders and reaching for the wall again.

An enormous, green tail flew out of the water and slammed into her, flinging her half way across the watery pit.

A moment later, Scott was snatched from underneath Tom, just as Tom snagged his fingers on the tip of the stone snake's tip.

As Tom dangled by his fingertips, Scott vanished beneath the water.

"Scott!"

Leandro saw Tom hanging from the slide and raced over to him. But as he clutched Tom's foot to try to climb up, Ella appeared, tearing at Leandro's shoulders, shredding his flesh to clamber over him and climb up Tom.

With all the strength he could muster, Tom held on tight as Ella clawed her way up his back, leaving Leandro behind. Meanwhile, all Tom could do was look down at the dark splashing waters, screaming, "Scott!"

As Ella pulled herself up and over Tom and began to precariously pull herself up the steep stone slide, Scott was hurled through the air, crashing into Leandro, who was still trying to clamber up Tom's leg.

Leandro lost his grip, and both he and Scott splashed into the water.

They broke the surface together, choking for air, when out of the water before them rose the head of the green anaconda, the largest snake on the planet. It reared its head high, leering at Scott and Leandro, looking from one to the other, its huge tongue flicking in and out of its lipless mouth, smelling the fear in the pit.

Almost tasting it.

Ready to devour it.

Suddenly, the *thump-thump-thump* of chopper blades came from above.

A torrent of downdraft filled the pit.

A second later, a rope ladder unfurled from the daylight above, descending all the way into the chamber until it splashed into the water beside Leandro.

The moment it landed, Leandro made a desperate grab for the ladder.

But his sudden movement was enough to cost him his life.

As his fingers latched onto the rungs, the anaconda lunged and latched onto him.

Leandro screamed as the snake dragged him into the water for the last time, its gigantic, powerful body now looping around his torso, crushing his bones.

As Leandro's screams echoed up the pit, Ella made a desperate leap from the snake slide to the rope ladder, clutching on tight and climbing upward as fast as she could.

Scott shouted to Tom, "Jump!"

Tom leaped for the ladder, grabbing on tightly before shouting back down at Scott, "What about you?"

But Scott was already rushing through the water as fast as he could for the ladder. He took the rungs in his fists and hurried up behind Tom. He paused and glanced back once, watching as the giant anaconda thrashed through the water, pulverizing every last bone and organ in Leandro's body before opening its mouth wide and taking the Brazilian's head into its jaws—

—while he was still barely alive.

"There goes the map," Scott said to himself, knowing the map was still in Leandro's pocket, realizing now only too well how determined the Amazon was to keep her secrets.

Up above him, Ella reached daylight and was pulled to safety, followed by Tom.

As Scott reached the top of the ladder, he saw through the temple entrance the helicopter sitting between the temple and the ravine, its rotor blades still whirring.

He saw the rope ladder stretching all the way from the edge of the pit to the chopper.

He saw Ella standing over him, drenched but still with that smug grin on her face.

And he saw Oscar Hudson standing beside her, holding Tom at gunpoint.

"Well, well, well," the murderous billionaire said, smiling down at Scott as he reached the top of the ladder. "Look what the anaconda dragged in."

Chapter XIII

Rio de Janeiro, Brazil

From the stark surroundings of Oscar Hudson's concrete and glass mansion set 600 feet high in the sheer cliff face of *Morro da Urca*, Scott and Tom could see the storm rolling toward them through the night. Lightning flared over Guanabara Bay. The wind blew hard against the floor-to-ceiling window that spanned the room. Thunder cracked and rumbled ominously before the storm announced its arrival with a fierce sheet of rain slamming against the glass.

A few feet from the window, Scott and Tom each sat in a chair, their backs to one another and their hands tied together behind them.

Ella stood a short distance away, pouring two glasses of champagne before putting the bottle down beside a closed briefcase sitting flat on the long marble dining table. On the floor beside the table was Ella's backpack, the emerald orchid still inside. Scott had barely taken his eyes off it since they arrived at the mansion.

Ella had noticed. "What a shame it'll never be yours," she

said tauntingly. "But don't worry. I'll be sure to think of you every time I look at it. Your memory will live on, long after you're gone. What a pity it's not made of sapphire."

She laughed and took one of the glasses of champagne to her father who was standing at the head of the table, his eyes fixed on the glass cylinder in his hands.

Through a thin veil of freezing mist, he looked at the tiny green Qixoto orchid inside.

"Incredible," he whispered in complete awe of his specimen. "How something so beautiful, so small, will soon become the most powerful substance on the planet."

"Here, I have something for you to help celebrate," said Ella, handing Oscar his glass of champagne.

Oscar smiled. "And I have something for you," he said to his daughter. Oscar nodded toward the briefcase on the table. "It was supposed to be for Leandro, a little reward for his efforts. But now he's no longer with us, I thought you should have it. Go ahead, open it."

Excitedly, Ella made her way toward the briefcase.

She unfastened the latches and lifted the lid.

Her eyes lit up at the sight of money—piles and piles of it—all U.S. dollars stacked neatly inside. "How much is it?" she asked.

"Five hundred thousand," Oscar said. "Buy yourself something nice. A handbag, an African safari, anything you like."

Ella smiled. "Perhaps I'll go on an African safari and shoot myself a handbag."

"That's my girl."

From across the room, Scott rolled his eyes. "Like daddy, like daughter," he said. "You two really make a fine pair."

Ella crossed the room back to Oscar, and with her eyes still fixed on Scott, she planted her lips on her father.

Scott screwed up his face. "I take it back. You make the *perfect* pair... of psychos."

Oscar sighed impatiently and checked his watch. "You have precisely... five minutes left to insult us all you like, Mr. Sapphire. After that, I'm afraid I'll be leaving you in the capable hands of my daughter."

"I have a feeling she won't be offering us a glass of that Dom Perignon," Scott commented.

"How perceptive of you," Oscar said. "No, she won't. While I take the helicopter—and the orchid—directly to our laboratories in Sao Goncalo, Ella is going to finish the two of you off once and for all, and make certain your remains are as difficult to find as my precious orchid. Only there won't be a map to find you."

With that, Oscar Hudson planted one last kiss on his daughter before taking the cylinder and leaving the room.

Instantly, Ella turned her sinister smile toward Scott and Tom.

Outside the window, a bolt of lightning split the sky.

Ella set her champagne glass down on the table, reached into the backpack on the floor, and retrieved her gun before strutting confidently over to her captives, standing dominant and spread-legged before Scott.

She eyed his bare chest and raised one eyebrow. "It's a shame, you know. I would have liked to have seen you both tortured for a little while first. But that was more Leandro's forte. He was very good with a knife. Almost like a surgeon."

"Which is pretty much what it'll take to get him out of that anaconda, don't you think?" Scott said. "At least, what's left of him."

Ella didn't take kindly to the remark.

With as much force as she could muster, she slapped Scott hard across the face.

His head reeled to the right before he shook the slap off, flexing his jaw to make sure it wasn't broken. Thunder shook the mansion.

"As sexy as you are, you're beginning to grate on me, Mr.

Sapphire."

"Trust me, there's not a single part of me that wants to grate on you."

Ella's hand cut the air once again, slapping Scott even harder across the face.

Scott blinked his eyes madly and shook his head before refocusing on Ella. "That's some arm you've got there. Are you sure you're not a man?"

Ella struck Scott one last time.

This time, she split his lip and sent a splash of blood across the floor.

As the rain and wind pounded against the window and another streak of lightning flashed through the sky, Ella leaned forward and shoved her face as close to Scott as she could.

"I'm going to kill your boyfriend first and make you watch," she whispered.

"I've got my back to him," Scott whispered back. "You'll have to spin me around so I can see."

"My pleasure."

Ella grabbed the legs of Scott's chair to swivel him around, but the second she did so, Scott lifted his feet up into Ella's chest and kicked as hard as he could.

Ella gasped as Scott launched her backward into the air.

Her body flew across the room.

Her arm flailed, pointing with the gun as she fired off a single bullet.

Her aim was wide.

The bullet shattered one of the floor-to-ceiling panes, and suddenly the room filled with shards of glass carried in by the torrent outside.

Ella fell against the table, her head striking the marble as rain and wind filled the room, bringing the storm inside.

The money in the suitcase suddenly took flight, each and

every note flapping through the room in a blinding flurry as though a blizzard had struck.

Thunder crashed.

Lightning flashed.

Scott looked at the drenched, glass-covered floor and shouted to Tom, "Left! Go left!"

Instantly, Tom threw himself left while Scott threw himself to the right, the two managing to tip their chairs over and slam to the floor. Scott felt a shard of broken glass near his hand. He snatched it up with his fingertips and started cutting through the rope that bound his and Tom's hands together.

Across the floor, Ella stirred groggily at the foot of the table, blood running down her face. She opened her eyes to see the whirlwind of money flying through the air. "No!" she screamed, watching as the storm blew through the shattered window while her money was sucked outside.

Scott cut through the rope.

He and Tom pulled their arms free and climbed to their feet.

Ella realized her gun was still in her hand.

She aimed it at Scott and fired—

—but Tom was the one who took the bullet, pushing Scott out of the way as the shot hit Tom square in the shoulder.

As Tom fell, Scott dropped to his knees on the wet floor underneath Tom and caught him.

"Tom," he gasped.

"I'm okay," Tom uttered, his breath catching before he looked Scott in the eye. "We have to stop Oscar Hudson."

"We will," Scott promised. "Just stay down while I take care of this bitch!"

As Ella raised her gun to fire again, Scott charged at her through the squall of flying cash and crashed straight into her. Together, they slammed onto the top of the marble table and skidded across its now soaked surface.

The gun toppled from Ella's hand onto the floor, skidding toward the shattered window and the storm outside.

With both hands free, she pushed Scott off the top of her and tumbled off the table toward the gun.

At the same time, Scott snatched up the bottle of Dom Perignon still sitting on the table and rolled onto the floor.

Ella grabbed the gun, jumped to her feet and aimed the weapon toward Scott.

But Scott was already in front of her, swinging the bottle of champagne at her as he shouted, "This is for killing Dr. Osvaldo."

The heavy bottle slammed against Ella's face with a dull *thunk*!

She staggered backward toward the shattered window as Scott swung again.

"This is for saving your life when it was the last thing I wanted to do."

The second blow sent Ella reeling backward even further, the storm blowing into the room from behind her as she teetered toward the window.

"And this," Scott said through clenched teeth, "is for shooting Tom!"

With one final blow, Scott struck Ella with the champagne bottle so hard that her heels began sliding on the wet polished concrete floor.

Her body stumbled backward.

And as a bolt of lightning lit up the sky, Ella Hudson screamed and fell backward out through the shattered window, falling 600 feet down the cliff face to her doom as the storm swallowed the echoes of her final scream.

Scott watched her vanish into the night before turning back to Tom.

As money continued to spin and spiral through the room, Scott slid to his knees beside Tom who was already pulling himself up.

"Oscar," he said determinedly. "We need to stop Oscar."

"No. You stay here," Scott said.

But Tom shook his head. "He killed my father. I'm not stopping now."

Scott knew from the look on his face that this was something Tom had to do. He helped him to his feet and together they raced out of the room—

—but not before Scott snagged the backpack containing the emerald orchid and hoisted it over one shoulder.

As Scott and Tom pushed open the door to the rooftop of the mansion they were met with the full fury of the storm and the downdraft of the helicopter's whirring rotors sending tornadoes of rain and wind swirling across the rooftop.

With a bounce and a precarious pitch left, and then right, the chopper negotiated the violent winds and began to lift off. Scott and Tom could see Oscar in the pilot's seat, his face lit up in the glow of the instrument panel.

But as the chopper began to lift off and veer about, Oscar failed to catch sight of both Scott and Tom sprinting across the rooftop toward the ascending chopper.

Tom launched himself into the air first, undaunted and determined to stop Oscar at any cost. With his one good arm he latched onto the left landing skid of the chopper.

The chopper tilted down to the left.

Oscar pulled on the controls, thinking the wind had caught him. He overcompensated and tilted the bird to the right—unwittingly allowing Scott the chance to leap into the air and grab hold of the right landing skid.

Suddenly, an updraft caught the chopper and lifted it high into the sky.

Oscar eyed the glass cylinder tucked safely into a pouch in the passenger door of the helicopter. As another growl of thunder roared across the sky, he steered the chopper up and over the peak of *Morro da Urca*, flying the bird over the cable car stations on the lower peak. Lightning lit up the night and he could see the lines of the cables stretching up toward the higher peak of Sugarloaf Mountain.

The cable cars had stopped running earlier in the night.

Now, as lightning lit up the sky, he could see the empty cable cars swinging and swaying on the cables, a hundred or so feet apart, all the way up to the peak of Sugarloaf.

Oscar began to take the chopper higher when suddenly the right rear passenger door of the chopper slid open.

The storm blew in, and Oscar struggled to maintain control of the helicopter.

That's when the left rear passenger door slid open.

"What the fuck?" Oscar cursed as the helicopter started to spin and swirl over the cables running from one mountaintop to the other.

He glanced back to see Scott clambering into the chopper from one side and Tom climbing on board from the other.

Oscar quickly reached under the pilot's seat and pulled out a gun.

He swung it behind him, aiming recklessly and pumping off a bullet in Scott's direction.

Scott ducked, landing on top of the rolled-up rope ladder as the bullet shot off into the storm.

A second later, Tom grabbed Oscar from behind, seizing him in a headlock and snarling into Oscar's ear, "You killed my father. Now it's your turn to die."

Suddenly, Oscar let go of the controls.

The helicopter banked into a dive.

At the same time, Oscar threw his fist backward, breaking the bridge of Tom's nose and dropping him to the floor.

As Oscar snatched control of the chopper once again, he tilted it left.

A semi-conscious Tom rolled toward the open rear door.

Scott reached for him fast, grabbing hold of Tom's shoulder just before he rolled out the open door. "Tom! Wake up!"

Bleary-eyed, his nose bleeding, Tom shook himself awake at the sound of Scott's voice.

He smiled at Scott.

And Scott smiled back.

And in his groggy, wounded, bleeding state, Tom said, "I think I love—"

Oscar banked the bird left again, sharper than before.

This time, before Scott had time to grab for him—

—Tom disappeared out the open rear door.

Scott gasped.

He dived for the door, looking out into the storm to see Tom falling—

—and slamming onto the roof of one of the swinging cable cars directly below them.

As the storm rocked the car, Scott could see Tom grabbing on tight to the roof, dazed and disoriented.

Another bullet was fired from behind Scott, shooting out through the open cabin of the chopper as Oscar struggled to maintain control of the whirling helicopter and shoot at Scott at the same time.

Laying low in the rear of the chopper, Scott kicked a boot straight into Oscar's face.

Oscar's head rolled back on his neck as he fired off one last bullet.

This time the bullet missed the open door.

It hit the back of the chopper's fuselage, ricocheted off the ceiling and slammed straight into the helicopter's control panel in the shower of sparks.

The shrill sound of warning alarms filled the cabin.

The chopper spun into a downward spiral, circling the

swinging cable car to which Tom clung desperately in the storm.

Oscar dropped the gun and gripped the controls with both hands.

In the rear of the cabin, Scott glanced out the open door, the entire world spinning as thunder crashed, lightning cracked and the blades of the out-of-control chopper whined and howled.

At a glance, Scott saw Tom atop the swaying cable car.

Quickly, he looked around the cabin and saw the rolled-up rope ladder.

With a kick, he sent the ladder unfurling into the storm.

As the chopper spiraled through the sky, descending toward the cable car, the end of the ladder slammed down next to Tom. He glanced up at the out-of-control chopper. Instantly, he knew there was no way Scott could climb down to safety.

No, he knew that Scott had another plan.

Tom seized the end of the ladder just before it slid off the roof of the cable car—

—and prayed that he knew exactly what Scott was thinking.

The chopper whirled violently through the sky.

Inside the rear of the cabin, Scott unfastened the top of the ladder from the latches fixed to the chopper floor. He wrapped the end of the rope ladder around his arm as tight as he could as could while the chopper swirled like a hurricane through the storm.

At the same time, Tom held onto the roof rigging of the swinging cable car and hauled on the end of the ladder, wrapping it around the rigging as tight as he could.

A downdraft pushed the chopper into a nosedive.

Oscar gasped, knowing now there was no way of saving the helicopter—or himself.

But if he was going to die—

—he was taking Scott Sapphire with him.

As the chopper plunged from the sky, past the swinging cable car, Oscar reached back and grabbed Scott's leg. And with a smile he said, "Sorry, but it's time for us to die... together!"

But Scott coiled the end of the ladder around his arm even tighter, the backpack still slung over his shoulder, and shook his head. "Sorry, but it's time for you to die... alone!"

Suddenly, the ladder jerked tight, and as the helicopter continued to fall—

—Scott was yanked out through the open door of the chopper.

As the rope ladder swung in the wind and rain, Scott held on tight.

The other end of the knotted ladder snapped tight on the rigging.

The ladder swung like pendulum as Scott looked up at the rocking cable car above—

—and then down at the helicopter plummeting toward the ground, its blades whirring, draining out Oscar Hudson's furious screams until—

KABOOM!

The chopper hit the ground far below in a fiery explosion.

A fireball rose into the sky, quickly extinguished by the rain and wind.

But Scott was no longer looking down.

He was looking up.

Up the length of ladder he had to climb—

—to the face peering over the edge of the cable car's roof—

—one hand already extended down toward him, beckoning him to climb.

And as the wind twirled and tossed the ladder, Scott did exactly that.

He climbed.

When he reached the roof of the cable car, Tom pulled him to safety.

And pulled him into a kiss from which there was no escape.

A kiss that—amid the squall and the lightning and the thunder—Scott happily surrendered to.

When Scott eventually pulled out of that kiss, still panting, still relieved, he looked at Tom with a smile and said, "Fuck, I need a chocolate."

Chapter XIV

Yorkshire, England

The old black English cab drove along the long driveway to the 17th century mansion.

In the backseat, Tom—with one arm in a sling from his gunshot wound and a bandage across the bridge of his nose—kissed Scott once again before glancing out the window at their destination.

"I have to admit, I'm kinda nervous about meeting your family."

"Why?" Scott asked.

Tom gestured out the window as they approached the centuries old manor. "Look where they live."

"Oh," Scott said, peering out the window. "Well, looks can be deceiving." To change the subject he asked, "Do you remember what you started to tell me in the helicopter?"

"You mean, just as I fell out the door, and you didn't catch me?"

"Yeah, just as you fell out, and I didn't catch you. So inconsiderate of me, I know."

Tom looked at Scott teasingly. "Geez, I can't remember. I had a blow to the head. I'm really not sure. Maybe you could help jog my memory."

Scott leaned in and kissed him, his tongue pushing passionately between Tom's lips.

"Oh, maybe now I remember," Tom said, taking his time. "It was something like, 'I think I—"

Suddenly, the cab pulled up at the entrance of the mansion as the driver leaned back and said, "Here we are, gents! Mighty impressive house you got here."

Tom grinned at Scott, his sentence still teasingly unfinished.

Scott leaned forward to the cab driver and handed him a fifty. "Would you mind waiting here for us?"

Tom looked confused. "I thought I was meeting your family?"

"You are," Scott smiled, before whispering reassuringly, "Quick getaways are always a good idea to plan in advance."

"Quick getaways?" Tom asked, concerned.

Scott nodded. "They run in the family."

He and Tom left the cab, but not before Scott grabbed the backpack on the back seat.

They found Artie and Sophie taking high tea in the garden terrace that extended from the left wing of the mansion.

"Well, I have to say this place is one of my favorites," Scott said, announcing his arrival.

Artie gasped with excitement at the sight of Scott, spluttering up his tea with a "Blimey! Are we glad to see you! Welcome home!" Artie gestured to a tray of *Doux Baiser* Belgian chocolates on the table. "We've got your favorites!"

At the same time, Sophie simply *squeed* before grabbing her elbow crutches to slip and hobble her way into Scott's arms. He caught her seconds before her excitement sent her toppling, wrapping her in a muscle-bound embrace as he spun her around on the spot.

"God, I've missed you!" she said. "Are you okay?"

"I'm better than okay," he said, settling her back into her crutches before popping one of the chocolates into his mouth with a sigh of pleasure. He ate the chocolate for courage, then took a deep breath and said, "I have someone I want you to meet."

Artie and Sophie turned their attention to the man with his arm in a sling lingering a short, nervous distance behind Scott.

"Artie and Sophie, I'd like you to meet Tom. Tom, this is Artie and Sophie."

Graciously, Tom stood forward and said to Artie in his Texan accent, "Sir, I have all the respect in the world for your son." He turned to Sophie and added, "And may I say, you are as beautiful as your brother is handsome. And might I add, your house is nothing short of... well... astonishing."

Sophie was the first to step forward and shake Tom's hand. "It's a pleasure to meet you, Tom. You seem very sweet. Although, I'm not Scott's real sister. But we are family."

Tom glanced at Scott, a little confused.

"It's okay," Scott said. "We're just a different kind of family, that's all."

"That we are," Artie said, strutting forward to shake Tom's hand as pretty little sparrows began to flit and splash in the birdbath in the middle of the terrace. He turned to Scott and asked, "So? Is the emerald real?"

With a smile on his face, Scott reached into the backpack and slowly pulled out the emerald orchid.

Brilliant green shards of light glittered in Artie's eyes as Scott handed it to him.

"Oh, my," Artie breathed, delicately talking hold of the treasure. "You've done well."

"And I want the money to go back to the preserving the Amazon," Scott said. "I promised someone it would go back to where the orchid came from."

Artie nodded respectfully. "That's a good promise. Sophie and I have already arranged a private auction. At a suite at the Dorchester in London. The bidders have all signed a confidentiality agreement. Although, we may need you to take the call from a silent bidder," he said to Scott.

"Sure," Scott said. "I can do—"

Before he could finish his sentence, the sound of dogs barking and snarling filled the air.

Getting closer.

Growing more and more vicious.

Barking and snarling, louder and louder.

Artie grinned and put down his teacup. "Time to go!"

Tom looked at Scott, confused. "What's going on?"

But Scott was already scooping Sophie up in his arms, telling Tom, "Grab Artie. Get to the cab! Now!"

As the four of them raced down the steps of the terrace and bolted for the waiting cab, six huge black Doberman guard-dogs came tearing around the corner of the estate, frothing at the mouth.

Scott, Sophie, Tom, and Artie raced for the cab still waiting in the driveway of the mansion.

Artie leaped in the front passenger seat as Scott threw Sophie into the backseat before he and Tom clambered inside.

"Drive!" Scott shouted, his door still open.

As the first of the jaw-snapping Dobermans raced toward them, the cab took off just as Scott slammed his door shut.

With an exhilarating laugh, Artie said, "God, I love it!"

Tom looked at Scott, panting and confused.

Scott simply laid his hand on Tom's knee, planted a kiss on his lips, and said, "Welcome to the family."

Chapter XV

The Dorchester Hotel, London

The emerald orchid sat on the stand at the front of the small, private suite.

In secrecy, they had gathered.

European baronesses and Wall Street tycoons.

Dotcom entrepreneurs and Shanghai art collectors.

British rockstars and Brunei royalty.

The small crowd sat in chairs facing the priceless emerald as Artie set aside his sometimes rough manner and put on his best show. "Do I hear an opening bid for this extraordinary jewel saved from the wilds of the Amazon?"

A Norwegian investor raised his hand. "One million dollars."

Immediately, a Saudi businessman called, "Five million."

On a cell phone in a corner of the room, Scott was talking to a silent bidder. A woman. "The current bid is five million," he informed her.

In a distinctly Eastern European accent, the silent bidder calmly said, "Ten million."

Scott raised his hand and mouthed 'ten' to Artie.

A Dubai princess jumped in with with fifteen.

The Saudi businessman upped his bid to twenty.

The Norwegian investor discreetly bowed out while Scott announced, "Thirty," for his silent bidder.

The Saudi businessman jumped up and stubbornly announced, "Forty!"

The Dubai princess announced, "Fifty!"

With a smile on his face and the phone in his hand, Scott mouthed 'sixty' to Artie.

The Dubai princess suddenly clutched her Louis Vuitton bag, signaled to her entourage, and stormed out of the suite.

Before the door slammed, the Saudi businessman shouted "Seventy-five million. And that is my final bid!"

A wave of excited whispers spread through the suite as Scott stood, the phone pressed to his ear, listening for his final instruction.

He nodded.

He looked to Artie.

And he smiled.

"One hundred million dollars."

In an uproar the Saudi businessman jumped to his feet and threw his chair across the room. Bidders stormed from the suite, stunned and shocked and slamming the door one after another.

As the billionaire bidders left the private suite one by one, Scott said to his silent bidder, "Congratulations. You won. The emerald is yours."

But with a flat tone the bidder on the phone replied, "I don't want it. All I wanted was to find you, Mr. Sapphire."

Scott's brow instantly creased in concern. "Who are you?"

"My name is Tatyana Romanov. And you lost my Golden Egg. Something that is more precious than you realize."

"What do you want?" Scott breathed quietly into the phone.

There was a pause before Tatyana answered, "I want you to

retrieve the egg and deliver it to me in Moscow within one week. Or else—"

"Or else what?"

"Or else your friends Sophie and Tom—the two you left in the suite across the hall from you at the Dorchester—will die."

With that, the phone went dead.

With that, Scott charged from the suite, into the hallway, and shouldered open the door to the room opposite.

The curtains billowed on the breeze of the smashed-open balcony doors.

Chairs and tables had been upturned.

Sophie's elbow crutches lay strewn across the floor.

And Tom and Sophie—

—were gone.

As Artie raced into the room behind Scott, panting and panic-stricken, he desperately asked, "Oh, God, where's Sophie? Where's Tom?"

A tear spilled down Scott's cheek.

And all he could answer was—

"Russia."

COMING SOON

SCOTT SAPPHIRE
AND THE GOLDEN EGG

Russia. A country with a history of uprisings and upheavals. A land of royal bloodlines and bloody revolutions. And keeper of the most sought-after secret known to humankind.

The Elixir of Life.

There is only one map on the planet that leads to the Elixir...

There is only one woman who knows where that map is...

And Tatyana Romanov—descendant of Czar Nicolas II—has gone to extreme measures to ensure that the one man in the world who can obtain that map delivers it to her...

...before one of history's most notorious villains rises up once more to stop anyone from discovering his secret.

From the French Riviera to Moscow's Red Square, from Russia's bloody past to a discovery that could change the future of humankind forever, Scott Sapphire will stop at nothing to save his friends and find... the Golden Egg.

About the Author

From palace-hopping across the Rajasthan Desert to sleeping in train stations in Bulgaria, from spinning prayer wheels in Kathmandu to exploring the skull-gated graveyards of the indigenous Balinese tribes, Geoffrey Knight has been a traveler ever since he could scrape together enough money to buy a plane ticket. Born in Melbourne but raised and educated in cities and towns across Australia, Geoffrey was a nomadic boy who grew into a nomadic gay writer. His books are the result of too many matinee movies in small-town cinemas as a child, reading too many Hardy Boys adventures, and wandering penniless across too many borders in his early adult life. He currently works in advertising and lives in Paddington, Sydney. And can't wait to buy his next plane ticket.

Other Works by Geoffrey Knight

The Cross of Sins
The Riddle of the Sands
The Curse of the Dragon God
Drive Shaft
Drive Shaft 2: Between a Rock and a Hard Place
The Gentlemen's Parlor: Room of Chains
Under the Bridge
The Pearl Trilogy
To Catch a Fox
The Boy from Brighton
Hotel Pens
Paperboy: Boys of Perfection
Nude Surfing
The Declaration
Video Store Valentine
Together in Electric Dreams
Harm's Way
On the Overgrown Path
Why Straight Women Love Gay Romance

Anthologies

Best Gay Erotica 2013
On Valentine's Day

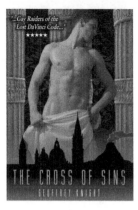

...Gay Raiders of the
Lost DaVinci Code...
★★★★★

THE CROSS OF SINS
GEOFFREY KNIGHT

Somewhere in the world is a statue so sinful that a secret sect of the Church wants it destroyed at any cost. Somewhere in the Turkish desert, in the streets of London, and in the depths of Venice, are the clues to find it. And, somewhere in the hearts of five sexy, daring, thrill-seeking gay men, is the courage and die-hard determination to unravel one of the greatest mysteries of all time.

Meet Luca da Roma, an Italian model and expert in art, both ancient and modern; Dr. Eden Santiago, Brazilian biologist, physician and genetic engineer; Shane Houston, a Texas cowboy and an expert in cartography; Will Hunter, a San Diego college student and football star, majoring in ancient history; and Jake Stone, an adventurer-for-hire from New York and the newest member of Professor Fathom's team of hot gay adventure seekers.

Now available from Storm Moon Press!
Digital: $6.49/Print $13.99

Connor Smith works for Primrose, an organization tasked with monitoring and tracking aliens and alien technology. It's a job that doesn't know the meaning of "nine-to-five". It also doesn't leave much room for a social life, a complication that Connor hasn't minded, until now. At the prodding of his best friend, Connor reluctantly puts himself back in the dating pool, even though it means lying about his remarkable life.

Elsewhere, Noah Jones has led a remarkable life of his own. Stranded on Earth in 1648, Noah was forced to transform himself permanently into human form to survive. He soon learned that in doing so, he'd become effectively immortal, aging only at a glacial pace. Alone, with no way to contact his people or return home, Noah becomes a silent observer of human civilization—always in the world, but never of the world. Then, hundreds of years later, he sees a face in a crowd and instantly feels a connection that he thought he'd never feel again. But he's too late: Connor's already taken.

Destiny is not without a sense of humor, though, and the two men are pulled inexorably closer, snared by the same web of dangers and conspiracies. Worse, Primrose is now aware of Noah, and they aren't ones to leave an alien unrestrained. So while Connor struggles to understand the strange pull he feels toward Noah, forces without as well as within are working against them to keep them apart.

Power in The Blood

Angelia Sparrow

Oren Stolt understands the natural order better than most people. Vampires prey on humans and Undying keep the vampires' numbers in check.

Until now.

Now, across the United States, vampire numbers are exploding, thanks to a new church. The Tabernacle of the Firstfruits preaches a Risen Lord and invites believers to follow Him in death and resurrection... quite literally.

In Memphis, the church is about to host its first conference, with an eye to converting the whole world to the vampiric gospel.

And all that stands between humanity and eternal night is Oren, his kids, and a thin line of insane immortals.

Now available from Storm Moon Press!
Digital: $5.99/Print: $9.99

CPSIA information can be obtained at www.ICGtesting.com
Printed in the USA
LVOW04s1612240814

400622LV00005B/537/P